"You Should've Let Me Know About Our Baby."

"You're not coming into our lives now, Jared. Forget that. I don't see that you have any rights in the matter."

"Understand me, Megan, I intend to get to know my son," he declared, his temper rising. He clenched his fists and inhaled deeply.

In spite of all his anger, he wanted her. She was as beautiful and enticing as she was infuriating. He desired her and he wished she would cooperate with him—both impossibilities.

"I see no point in arguing further," she said.

"Megan, I will get to know Ethan. That's a fact, not a wish."

She clamped her lips closed for a moment. "I know you've had a shock. But don't tear up Ethan's life. You'll only hurt him if you come into his life. You'll raise a hundred questions."

"You should have thought of those questions," Jared said. "You should have known that this day would come."

Dear Reader,

Come along to the Northwest, the way three handsome billionaires have—right into romance.

Beginning with *Dakota Daddy,* three stories are heading your way about Western heroes. Each revolves around an irresistible, dashing billionaire. What could these daring moguls want enough to fight for? More money? Revenge? Love? All of these gave me an opportunity to develop my main characters in this first book. In doing so, I revisited a wonderful place I lived for five years, South Dakota. The story brought back memories of windswept open plains and gorgeous sunsets, as well as the crisp air of cooler summers and the friendly people. Into this background the story evolves when a sexy billionaire seeks payback and gets the shock of his life. Both he and the woman he once loved harbor secrets. While they try to exact retribution for old hurts, their stormy passions rekindle.

This is the first story of three affluent cousins who've made a bet that will take a year to resolve. Temporarily leaving Texas, the three are drawn north to their roots in South Dakota, Montana and Wyoming. With the wealth of dreams, the first story is Jared Dalton and Megan Sorenson's, star-crossed lovers who were torn apart earlier in their lives. With hopes and plans as big as the Western plains, their passion is as hot as the summer sun when these two battle. Their turbulent emotions reveal long-hidden secrets. Through the upheavals, attraction rages fiercely until Jared and Megan once again fall in love.

Curl up in a favorite spot, read and enjoy!

Sara Orwig

DAKOTA DADDY

SARA ORWIG

Published by Silhouette Books
America's Publisher of Contemporary Romance

 SILHOUETTE BOOKS

Recycling programs for this product may not exist in your area.

ISBN-13: 978-0-373-76936-0
ISBN-10:   0-373-76936-9

DAKOTA DADDY

Books by Sara Orwig

Silhouette Desire

Falcon's Lair #938
The Bride's Choice #1019
A Baby for Mommy #1060
Babes in Arms #1094
Her Torrid Temporary
  Marriage #1125
The Consummate Cowboy #1164
The Cowboy's Seductive
  Proposal #1192
World's Most Eligible Texan #1346
Cowboy's Secret Child #1368
The Playboy Meets His Match #1438
Cowboy's Special Woman #1449
††*Do You Take This Enemy?* #1476
††*The Rancher, the Baby*
  & the Nanny #1486

Entangled with a Texan #1547
**Shut Up and Kiss Me* #1581
**Standing Outside the Fire* #1594
Estate Affair #1657
†*Pregnant with the First Heir* #1752
†*Revenge of the Second Son* #1757
†*Scandals from the Third Bride* #1762
Seduced by the Wealthy Playboy #1813
‡*Pregnant at the Wedding* #1864
‡*Seduced by the Enemy* #1875
‡*Wed to the Texan* #1887
**Dakota Daddy #1936

††Stallion Pass
*Stallion Pass: Texas Knights
†The Wealthy Ransomes
‡Platinum Grooms
**Stetsons & CEOs

SARA ORWIG

lives in Oklahoma. She has a patient husband, who will take her on research trips anywhere from big cities to old forts. She is an avid collector of Western history books. With a master's degree in English, Sara has written historical romance, mainstream fiction and contemporary romance. Books are beloved treasures that take Sara to magical worlds, and she loves both reading and writing them.

With love to Hannah, Rachel, Ellen,
Elisabeth, Colin, Cameron and Maureen

Prologue

"May the best man win!" Jared Dalton declared as the three cousins stepped out of a limousine into the bright Houston sunshine. Waiting on the tarmac were three sleek jets with each man's logo proclaiming ownership.

"One year from today, whoever's net worth increases the most wins our bet." Chase Bennett said, rehashing their agreement.

"Yes, the deadline for our bet is the first Friday next May," Matt Rome confirmed. "We each put five million in the pot, so whoever wins gets a fifteen-million-dollar prize."

"Right," Jared nodded. "On top of poker winnings, Chase."

Chase grinned. "I was lucky this year. Guys, it's been great to be together again."

"Still best friends, still bachelors—maybe forever bachelors. This weekend together is necessity," Matt said.

All three shook hands. "So long, my two best cuz," Jared said, grinning.

"If nothing else, we'll see each other next at the family Christmas get-together," Jared added. "Stay cool." He boarded a white plane and sat by a window, watching his cousins' planes taxi, one Houston-based cousin heading off to Paris, the other returning home to Wyoming. With mothers who were sisters, they had grown up close, even competing in football in college. All were wealthy and owner-CEOs of vast enterprises.

Jared intended to win the bet Matt had dreamed up. It would add some spice to work, akin to the thrill of success when he'd started out. Waiting until they were airborne, Jared withdrew his BlackBerry to send out messages that would start his staff searching for possibilities for solid moneymaking deals. He mulled over current projects and realized the bet gave him an opportunity for payback.

Excitement gripped him. He'd offer to buy the Sorenson ranch in Dakota. If Edlund Sorenson would sell, Jared could make money. Whether or not Edlund would sell, Jared knew he would have the satisfaction of letting an old enemy know he could buy him out. Making money was great. But best of all was revenge.

One

June

That old saying about a woman scorned was too damn true, Jared Dalton thought.

He thought back to when he'd first learned that old man Sorenson had died and that Megan had no apparent interest in keeping the family ranch. Jared assumed he could buy it easily. To his surprise, the minute Megan had learned who intended to buy the ranch, she'd withdrawn it from the market. Now he was here to get her to sell.

With a disturbing skip in his heartbeat that overrode a simmering anger, he saw Megan emerge from the Sorenson barn, carrying a saddle to the corral. She was too far away for him to see if her looks had changed. Her red shirt was as noticeable as her long-legged, sexy walk, which still revealed the years she had studied dance before she'd left for college. Her black hair was in a thick braid that lay on her back. Setting the saddle and blanket on the fence, she turned to the approaching horses to give each a treat. Within minutes she had saddled and mounted a sorrel.

The sight of her brought back too many hurtful memories. Vengeance was sweet. He just wished her father had lived to be part of the intended payback.

Jared intended to encounter her out on the ranch, where she would have to talk to him. He'd spent the night in a comfortable log guesthouse on her ranch without her knowledge in order to watch for her this morning. Before dawn he had dressed in jeans, a blue Western shirt and a wide-brimmed black Stetson.

Now he went to the barn to saddle a bay to follow her without haste.

The vast, grassy land made it easy to see in all directions except along the river, where trees could hide a rider from view. He knew he could catch her when she stopped at the river to let her horse drink. Until then, he didn't want to alert her that he was trailing behind. Thunder rumbled in the distance, and a glance at gathering clouds told him rain seemed imminent.

As soon as she reached the line of trees, she vanished from view. Watching, he could remember meeting her at the river—and their steamy kisses. Since their split, he rarely thought of her without bitter feelings surfacing.

Unwanted memories enveloped him. He had known her all his life. Even as their dads battled over water, he'd paid no attention to her because she had been six years younger—the skinny little kid on the neighboring ranch. The first time he'd ever noticed her was when he was getting his master's degree and she'd entered his same university in Chicago.

Too clearly he could recall that initial encounter. Her black hair had cascaded in a cloud over her shoulders and her startling turquoise eyes sped his pulse. She filled out a white cotton blouse that tucked into the narrow waistband of a tan skirt. When she'd smiled broadly at him and said hello, he'd thought he was looking at a stranger. If a beautiful woman greeted him, however, he had no intention of not responding.

"You don't know me, do you, Jared?"

Surprised, he'd stared at her and frowned, trying to recollect. "Did you go to UT?" he asked, referring to the University of Texas, where he'd gotten his undergraduate degree.

She laughed and stuck her tongue out at him and he sucked in his breath. All her pink tongue had done was make him think about kissing her. He was getting turned on and he didn't have a clue how he knew her.

"Jared, for heaven's sake!" she said. He shook his head, touching a lock of her soft hair.

"Okay, I give. I can't believe I don't remember a gorgeous woman. Where have we known each other?"

"I'm Megan Sorenson," she'd said, laughing at him. He stared in astonishment, seeing it now in the turquoise eyes. But that was all. Gone was the skinny little kid, replaced by a luscious, curvaceous woman.

"You grew up," he said, and that sparked a fresh burst of laughter.

"I didn't know you're going to school here," she said. "I thought I'd heard you'd graduated."

"MBA," he said slowly. "Have dinner with me tonight."

She tilted her head to study him. "You know how our dads fight. You and I should keep a distance."

"C'mon, Megan. Their fight isn't our fight. I've never in my life had anything against you."

"Oh, liar, liar!" she accused with amusement again dancing in her eyes. "You thought I was a pest. You wouldn't even say hello if you saw me."

He felt his face flush. "I'll make it up to you. I promise to give you my full, undivided attention," he said, and saw a flicker in her eyes. The moment between them sizzled and his heart raced.

"Dinner it is," she said breathlessly.

"About seven," he'd replied. And from that moment on, he'd thought he was in love. He'd hoped to marry her. They'd talked about it and planned on it, and then that summer after her freshman year, when Megan had gone to Sioux Falls to stay with her aunt and uncle, Olga and Thomas Sorenson, her dad sent one of his hands to summon Jared.

The old man had run him off by threatening harm to Jared's dad. He'd always wondered how much Megan had known about what her father was doing. For over a year he'd hurt, pain turning to anger that had grown when she wouldn't answer his letters. It pleased him enormously to buy her ranch. This payback was long overdue, and again he wished he'd offered to buy the ranch when Edlund Sorenson had still been alive, just to watch the old man's face.

Most obstacles weren't insurmountable, he'd discovered. Not with the wealth he had accumulated. He didn't expect this one to be, either.

He heard her horse before he rode into a clearing at the river's edge, and then he saw her. His insides clenched. Longing, hot and intense, rocked him. He rarely spent time on regrets but briefly, the thought that he never should have left her tore at him. Surprised, he shook aside his uncharacteristic reaction as she whirled around.

Color drained from her face. Her eyes widened until they were enormous and she swayed, making him wonder if she were about to faint. "Jared!" she exclaimed, as if he were an apparition.

"Megan, I didn't intend to startle you." He dismounted, dropping to the ground.

She drew herself up. As abruptly as she had looked on the verge of fainting, she pulled herself together.

Jared's heartbeat quickened at the sight of her. "You're more beautiful than ever," he said, and cursed himself with his next breath. Anger flashed in her turquoise eyes, those crystal-clear blue green eyes that were astonishing when he first looked at her.

"Why are you trespassing?" she asked, her composure obvious. He'd surely imagined her terrified reaction to the first sight of him. "This isn't your ranch, nor will it be. You get off my land."

"Whoa, give me a chance," he replied in amusement, reassessing changes in her. "Seven years was a long time ago."

"Not long enough. Your people were told this ranch is no longer on the market. I'm not selling. You'll never own this land." While thunder rumbled overhead, she withdrew a cell phone. "I don't know how you got one of my horses, but leave it where you found it and go. You're trespassing, and if you don't get off this ranch, I'm calling the sheriff."

"Don't be so emotional," Jared said, wishing he could unfasten her thick braid. "At least listen. You have nothing to lose."

Thunder boomed again, and she glanced skyward.

"I think, unless you don't mind getting soaked, you'll have to ride back to the barn with me," he added.

Without saying a word, she glared at him and then turned to mount her horse. Observing her tight jeans that pulled across an enticing bottom, Jared swung into the saddle as well, and waited for her to lead the way through the trees.

As the first large drops hit leaves overhead, they rode into the clearing. A jagged bolt of lightning flashed, and Jared knew they should get out of the open field and back to shelter.

He urged the bay he'd chosen, Jester, hoping she could keep up. Drops were coming faster by the time the barn loomed in sight.

As they galloped into the barn, the heavens opened. Jared dismounted, dropping to the ground while both horses shook their heads, sending drops flying.

To the accompaniment of the steady hiss of rain, they

unsaddled and rubbed down the horses. Once the animals were in stalls, Megan strode to the open door and watched the rain.

"Probably a summer shower. It'll move on," Jared said, standing close enough to catch the scent of an exotic perfume, not the rose perfume she once wore. "Why don't you listen to my proposition? I know you don't intend to retire to the ranch."

"You don't know that," she said, glancing up at him with hostility simmering.

"So you are?" he probed, and saw another flash of anger, knowing he had been correct.

"I am not selling my ranch to you," she said slowly and clearly. He looked at her mouth, remembering their kisses. She'd been eighteen years old then. What would it be like to kiss her now? "Why do you even want it? There are other ranches."

"I have a bet with my cousins, Chase and Matt, to see which one of us can increase his net worth the most during the coming year."

"My ranch is to help you win a bet?" she asked, glowering at him.

"That shouldn't make any difference to you."

"One more thing that you want for your own purposes," she said in a clipped tone.

"Whoever buys the place will purchase it for his own purposes," Jared said.

"I don't see how acquiring my ranch can put you over the top," she observed.

"That alone won't. It'll be one of several projects," he answered easily.

"How'd you get here and where did you get my horse?" she asked.

"If I had called you, I didn't think you'd take an appointment to talk to me about the ranch, so I sent one of my lawyers, Trent Colgin," Jared answered, and she compressed her lips.

"I should have known," she said. She rushed to yank up a horse blanket. "I'm going to the house. It could rain all day, and I don't intend to stay here. You get off the ranch however you got on it. Don't spend another night here, or I truly will call the sheriff."

"You're going to get soaked."

"That's better than staying here with you," she said and turned to dash for the sprawling ranch house. Jared ran easily beside her, not caring if he got wet as long as he could try to convince her to listen to him. They rushed up the back steps and across the wrap-around porch. While she draped the dripping blanket over a rocking chair, he pushed his hat to the back of his head.

In spite of the blanket, her jacket was soaked in the front and she shed it to hang it on another chair. Her damp shirt clung, revealing lush breasts that stirred erotic memories of kissing her as he caressed her breasts.

As she started to turn away, he looked into her eyes and suspected she guessed what he was thinking. His gaze trailed leisurely over her. Her quick breaths made her breasts thrust out more. When he looked up again, sparks flashed between them.

Raising her chin defiantly, she placed her hands on her hips. "I'm not inviting you inside."

"Megan, listen to what I have to offer. You may be losing a huge fortune. One you could make easily by getting rid of something you don't want anyway. You're letting emotion get in your way."

"I know what I want," she said with a frown.

"Try to keep an open mind. Come to dinner at my house tonight and let's discuss the sale."

"In this weather? I think not, thanks," she said, shaking her head.

"According to the paper, this rain is supposed to stop before noon and it won't rain again until tomorrow afternoon. Now quit spiting yourself and come have dinner with me. Why don't we discuss a deal? You have nothing to lose."

"I won't sell to you at any price," she snapped as she yanked a key out of her pocket and put it into the door.

"Scared to eat with me?" he asked softly in a taunting voice.

Her head came up and she faced him with anger blazing in her eyes, making them look more green than blue. "I'm not the least bit afraid of you," she replied in a haughty tone. "All right. I'll come to dinner, but you should know you won't change my mind."

"How's seven?"

"I'll be there."

"You know the way," he said, and her cheeks turned a deeper pink. "See you then." He left for his cabin, fighting the urge to glance to see if she stood watching him. He hadn't heard any door slam, but then in the rain, he probably wouldn't have.

* * *

She was coming for dinner, so there was hope. When hadn't he been able to talk a woman into something he wanted? She was beautiful, more poised than she'd been as a teen. Then, she had been friendly and warm as a kitten. Now she was a hellcat. Despite her anger, her self-confidence showed. She was not the naive, starry-eyed eighteen-year-old he had fallen in love with years ago.

Anticipation bubbled in him. How long before he could seduce her? he wondered. He planned to keep a clear sight on his goal of acquiring her ranch, but this new Megan was an unbearable temptation.

He packed his few things and drove back to his ranch to make arrangements for dinner. As if nature were cooperating, the rain ended by noon and sunshine broke out with a magnificent rainbow arching in the sky.

When he caught some news on the television, he went to his office to make a phone call to his cousin.

The minute Chase Bennett answered, Jared could picture his green eyes and easy smile. "Hi, Jared here. Just caught you on the news about oil you've found in Montana."

"Hope to find," Chase corrected. "If it pans out like I expect, it's going to be a tidy discovery."

"A bonus that it's in your home state," Jared remarked dryly.

"Yeah, but I don't spend much time back on the ranch," Chase replied.

"I'll wager you think you're going to win our bet," Jared joked, rubbing his finger on his knee as he talked.

"I hope to. You guys are going to have to get busy."

"I'm working on an interesting project. Remember Megan Sorenson? I plan to buy her ranch."

"Nice! That'll crush her dad. It will be satisfying to let him know you can buy him out."

"I wish I'd done this sooner. The old man died. As soon as Megan discovered I'm the buyer, she pulled the ranch off the market."

"Too bad. Making the offer should give you a bit of satisfaction. That would be a good purchase, a prime pheasant-hunting ranch, even though it won't help you win."

"Wait and see," Jared replied, chuckling, unwilling to reveal his plans to Chase. "Better go. Just called to offer congrats and tell you I still intend to collect."

"Dream on," Chase replied in a good-natured tone.

"I will," Jared said, and broke the connection, trying to be the one to get in the last word, a habit of the cousins since childhood. Jared gazed out the window. What to do about the Sorensen ranch…

The day seemed an eternity long, but eventually Jared showered, shaved and dressed with care in a tan knit shirt, chinos and hand-tooled leather Western boots that added to his six-foot-six height.

Promptly upon her arrival at seven, Jared met her on the porch. Watching her get out of her SUV and walk toward him, her slim column of a navy dress swirling around her shapely calves, he sucked in his breath. A large bow held the dress on her left shoulder, leaving the other shoulder bare. The material split as it fell from her shoulder, revealing her long legs as she walked. Her hair was rolled and fastened at the back of her head, giving her a sophisticated, self-possessed appearance. Had they gone out in public, she would have turned heads anywhere—the men in appreciation and speculation, women in envy and admiration.

Jared's pulse skipped, and he wondered if that bow on her shoulder released the front and back of her dress. He desired her with an intensity that shocked him. She was gorgeous, and momentarily he forgot the ranch, his purpose, old hurts, even anger. He saw a ravishing beauty whom he intended to seduce.

"Evening, Jared," she said. Her greeting brought him back to reality.

"You're stunning," he said in a deep, raspy tone, gazing into the cool, thickly-lashed turquoise eyes. "Welcome to my ranch," he added. "Come inside."

Without a word, she swept up the steps past him. When she passed, he caught that same exotic scent, a perfume he couldn't identify. Watching the slight sway of her hips, he followed her through the flagstone-covered entry into the wide front hall with its polished plank floor. She took his breath away with her beauty. He was reminded again that the open, outgoing warmth of the eighteen-year-old had deepened into the fieriness of a beautiful woman.

"I'm grilling steaks. Let's go to the patio," he suggested as he caught up to walk beside her.

She strolled in silence beside him outside to the patio, where smoke came from a large state-of-the-art stainless steel cooker. "You have all you need to live out here," she said, glancing around.

"Can I get you a glass of wine, tea, a soft drink? What's your preference?"

"White wine, please." She followed him to the bar, and he turned to hand a glass of pale wine to her. Even though their fingers brushed lightly, the contact was electrifying. He could feel the sparks, as close as he stood to her.

She tilted her head to study him. "You'll be returning to Texas soon, won't you?"

"It depends on what happens with you. I'm not in a hurry to go after seeing you again."

"Stop flirting, Jared. Or is that impossible?"

"Not impossible, but infinitely more interesting when you provoke it. How can I be with you and remain all business?"

"You might as well. The personal touch will get you nowhere."

He gave her a mocking smile. "Watch out, I might prove you wrong." He saw her gazing up at gray clouds streaking across the sky.

"When I crossed your river, the water was almost up to the bridge."

"Scared you'll get stranded with me?" he asked in amusement.

She whipped around to give him a level look. "No. I'll leave before I let that happen," she remarked.

"Here's to the future and forgetting the past," he said, ignoring her remark and raising his drink in a toast, even though he doubted he would ever lose all his bitterness toward her.

"This is pointless, Jared," she said, sipping her drink.

"Megan, we both did things that hurt. I left here and you married someone else two months later," he said, hoping he kept his tone casual enough to hide the stab that memory always brought.

"I'm sure you know my marriage didn't last much more than a month before we filed for a divorce," she replied with anger in her voice.

He recalled his fury and pain when his parents told him about a reception her father had for her and her new husband shortly after the marriage, and then the next thing he'd heard was that she was divorced, which gave him a degree of satisfaction.

"Where's your son from that marriage?" he asked, wondering about her child.

"With my aunt and uncle in Sioux Falls," she replied. A shuttered look had come over her features and he could feel a wall of coldness between them. She looked half angry, half afraid. He tried to curb his emotions and not let his bitter feelings interfere with his goals.

"At the time I couldn't stay to tell you why I was doing what I was doing," he said. "I never meant to hurt you like I did," he admitted quietly, refusing to get into it now, knowing she wouldn't listen to the truth about her father.

Twisting her shoulders out of his grasp, she strolled farther around the patio while he walked with her. "Jared, let's not rehash the past. As you said, it's done. Let go of it."

"I will if you will. But I know this is why you backed out of the deal we had for the ranch. Admit it,

you were ready and willing until you discovered that
I was the buyer."

"I'm not arguing with you about it. My dad would
have despised selling to you. I'll not do it—I promise
you," she said, her eyes wide and almost green again.

"Wait and let me talk to you about it, and what I'm
willing to pay," he said, fully confident he would win
her over.

"I agreed to tonight only. In the next hour over dinner
you can make your offer and then I'm out of your life."
Her gaze slid away from his, as if there were more she
wasn't saying. She'd hardly been reticent before. He
had a suspicious feeling there was something he was
missing, but he didn't know what.

"As far as leaving you alone—I don't know about
that. There's unfinished business between us."

"I can promise you, we won't renew it," she said with
such force he was taken aback. She walked on and he
stared after her. Again, he had been mystified by the
venom in her quiet tone. Why would she be that bitter
now? They had planned to marry, but he hadn't left her
at the altar. He'd never gotten that far—they'd talked
about marriage and getting engaged, and he was
looking for a ring for her when her father ruined their
plans. Her reactions were still strong enough for it all
to have happened last week instead of seven years ago.

"I'll check on dinner," he said, and went to the cooker.

Jared turned the steaks, watching her between glances
at his cooking. He wondered whether she was truly interested in her surroundings or simply trying to avoid him.

After turning the meat, he went into the house to get
things ready. Because of the threat of rain, they would

eat inside. If they had a real downpour, his bridge would be underwater and the ranch cut off.

Jared hoped to avoid any threat that would send her home early before he could convince her to sell. Revenge was his goal. He didn't want to return to Texas empty-handed, so he planned the kind of offer she couldn't turn down. This was a battle he wanted to win. And he hoped to have her in his arms tonight.

As he returned outside to get the steaks, she continued to circle the expansive patio. He observed her for a moment, aware how easy it was to watch her, letting his gaze drift slowly over her, recalling her passion and fire the night he had taken her virginity.

Pushing aside memories, he plated the steaks and joined her. "Dinner is served. I thought we'd eat inside— it's cozier."

"Fine," she said, smiling. "Although, 'cozy' isn't necessary to discuss business."

"You haven't smiled much. I like it."

"A smile changes nothing," she said, falling into step beside him.

He caught her arm and turned her to face him, holding both arms lightly. It was on the tip of his tongue to blurt out the truth to her about her father. Instead, Jared held back, knowing it might be a misguided sense of honor. Or not wanting to sound like he was making excuses. "Megan," he said solemnly, "admit it, all your hostility is a grudge because I walked out seven years ago. If that weren't between us, your father's fight with my father would no longer matter. It's solely about us. Right?"

Two

As Megan looked up at him, her heart drummed. "Yes, I hate you for that, Jared," she admitted reluctantly, hoping to get him out of her life with a desperation that was making a wreck of her nerves. This morning had shocked her beyond belief. She had almost fainted. She hated the light-headedness and queasy stomach the sight of him caused.

Even worse, she loathed the jump in her heartbeat, the unwelcome reaction he could still evoke effortlessly. He was more handsome and appealing than she remembered, and that cleft in his chin was even more noticeable to her now. Tall, dynamic, sexy—too many qualities that she couldn't ignore.

"I'm astonished you're even here. You have your chain of successful restaurants and you have high-rise

condos. I'm sure you have investments galore, plenty
to keep you busy."

"I'm interested in your ranch, and now in you. I'm
amazed you haven't married again," he said.

"Not so surprising," she replied carefully, her palms
growing sweaty with nervousness that she prayed she
hid. "I'm a divorced single mom. I'm young—six years
younger than you, if you recall. I haven't met the right
person. I've pursued a career."

"Why do I think you haven't touched on the real
cause," he broke in, and her pulse accelerated.

"I've given you all the explanations you'll ever hear,"
she said. In a taut moment, she was lost in his dark gaze.
When his gaze lowered to her mouth, her lips parted.
She hated the reaction she had to him, but she saw the
faint, mocking smile on his face. He knew what he
could do to her.

He ran his finger slowly along her jaw. "You know,
we could go at this a completely different way. We can
renew an old, solid friendship."

"Solid until you walked out without a word!" she
said, and yanked her head away, stepping back.
"There's nothing between us now. Jared, I—" she
began, tempted to get into her SUV and go.

"Let's eat," he interrupted, as if he guessed she was
on the verge of leaving. He walked away in long strides.
Distraught, with her heart pounding and her insides
churning, she watched him. Why was the past being
flung back in her face, when she had found some peace
and thought she was safe from having to deal with Jared?
If only he would leave. She couldn't wait to get through

dinner. The minute it was over she was going home, and, hopefully, he would go back to Texas forever.

In minutes, they were seated inside at a table, where thick, juicy steaks, steaming potatoes and crisp green salads awaited.

"Tell me about your life in Santa Fe. You have gallery now."

She smiled and sipped her water. "I suspect you already know a great deal about my life at home. I'd guess you have staff check on all pertinent details. Admit it, you could write a dossier on me. And you know what my home looks like, what my income is, what I drive. And you've seen pictures of my gallery."

"Actually, no," he replied, as she had his full, undivided attention. "Only pertinent facts. You're a potter living in Santa Fe with your son. You're single. You have your own gallery."

"That's about it," she said quietly, sipping ice water. "Santa Fe is an artists' colony, actually. It's a peaceful, thriving place, where someone can have a degree of privacy while maintaining an artist's public lifestyle. I prefer to keep it that way, Jared. You don't have to know about my life. Of course, you're in papers and magazines and the news often enough for any six people."

"That means nothing," he said.

"In the meantime, you've built a fortune on delicious dinners, with your exclusive Dalton's steak houses."

"I've been lucky. That first restaurant in Dallas was a far bigger success than I ever dreamed. You have to make reservations a month ahead at a Dalton's."

"Sounds impressive. You've had a spectacular rise."

He shrugged. "My dad bankrolled me with a huge sum of money, telling my brothers he would do the same for them when the time arrived. That hasn't been necessary. I made enough of a fortune that I brought my brothers into the business and we've never looked back."

"So what about your life and your offices and homes?"

He looked amused by her refusal to discuss herself. In spite of the polite conversation, they were sparring. She could feel the tension in the undercurrent, with his constant, unwanted appeal. So much about him was agonizingly familiar that it tore at her. Guilt, anger, desire pulling at her with increasing force. Dinner was eons long already, and they hadn't even gotten to the true purpose. She had lived with a secret for over six years now. Was she staying silent and committing a sin beyond measure?

She tried to focus on what he was saying about himself.

"I'm not anywhere half as interesting," he said. "I work and I play. The usual way. Mostly, I'm at my headquarters in Dallas, in meetings or on the phone. Depending on what's happening, I go out in the evening. Nothing exciting. I travel a lot, have no serious love life. Any men in your life right now?"

She wished she could answer yes and put another wall between them, but if he'd had staff check into her lifestyle, even minimally, Jared already knew the answer to his question. She shook her head. "No. I lead a busy life and my days are dedicated to my son first and my pottery second. They fill my hours."

"You're a beautiful, desirable woman," Jared remarked, his words slowing and his voice growing husky. "I find it difficult to think there's no one. It has to be your choice."

"Thank you," she replied, intending to answer briskly and move on, but her words came out breathless, far too revealing. "I suppose it's my choice, but my hours are taken. As it is, there aren't enough hours in the day."

Even though the steak was delicious, she had little appetite. Each bite was an effort. She was aware the evening had darkened early given the thunder, but she sat with her back to the windows.

"Tell me about Ethan," Jared said, startling her to hear him say her son's name.

"What's to say? He's a normal six-year-old. He plays soccer and T-ball. He has a mind for numbers, even at this age. He's tall and has my black hair."

"Where is he tonight?"

"In Sioux Falls with Aunt Olga and Uncle Thomas. Every summer when school is out, he stays with them for several weeks. You must know my parents died, but Uncle Thomas and Aunt Olga are like grandparents to him."

"Do you have joint custody?" he asked, startling her. She shook her head quickly.

"No. Mike wanted out of our marriage as much as I did. When he learned about a baby on the way, we were already divorced. He gave me full custody. He had no interest in Ethan. Ethan doesn't even know him."

"I can't imagine a man not wanting to know his own

son. Sorry," Jared said. "At least Ethan was too young to know what happened."

Thunder growled, rattling the windows and she glanced back. "I'd like to head home while it's not raining." She turned to look into Jared's dark eyes. "Let's get this over with. We might as well get to the main topic. My ranch is not for sale."

"Look at options," he said easily, leaning back in his chair. "You plan to stay in New Mexico, don't you?"

"Yes, I do, but as long as my aunt and uncle are alive, I have Dakota ties. They're close to Ethan, as I am with them."

"If you sell the place at the price I'm offering, you can afford your own plane and pilot, or charter a plane whenever you'd like to see them. That's not any reason to hang on to something that will be a burden. Your place will go to ruin if you don't care for it constantly."

"I'm aware of the problems," she said.

"Your uncle and aunt won't move out here?"

She shook her head. "No. They're city people and they have no interest in the ranch. I said I'd pay them to run it and give them a share in it, but they prefer to stay in Sioux Falls. Uncle Thomas and Dad never got along, and I don't think Uncle Thomas wants any part of the ranch. Their only son, Ralph, lives in D.C., and his wife's family is from Virginia, so he'll never come back here."

"So, why spend your money maintaining the ranch?" Jared asked. "Surely not out of spite. That's expensive and impractical."

"Our ranch is a profitable place, as you know. Which is exactly why you'd like it."

He shook his head. "It's profitable if it's run right. But you know your dad invested hours and money into it and made it what it is. You can't work in Santa Fe and maintain the ranch the way your dad did."

She knew Jared was right, but she wasn't going to admit it. She couldn't keep from feeling that if she refused him, he would go on to other things, and she could quietly find a buyer later in the year and sell without Jared knowing until it was a done deal.

"Are you willing to close your gallery and move back here?" Jared asked. He sounded as if he were asking a casual question. His quiet voice and easygoing manner were deceptive. Even though she hadn't been around Jared in years, she knew better. He had to care, and with his wealth, she suspected he was unaccustomed to rejection.

"I don't think I'll have to," she answered, with the same lightness of tone that he maintained. "If it turns out more of my time is required, I'll hire someone to run my gallery."

They both had stopped eating and she could feel the tension increase. She also realized the thunder was more frequent. "Jared, I have to get across your bridge."

"You have time," he said dismissively, and with as much certainty as if he controlled the weather, which, under other circumstances, would have amused her. "Here's what I'll do," he said. "I'll pay you one million more than your asking price of thirty million," he said flatly. "That has to be a figure that you have to consider."

Stunned, she stared at him. One million more was

huge. On top of her asking price, it was fantastic. "That's impressive," she said, studying him. "Why would you possibly want the Sorenson ranch that badly?"

He nodded. "Plus, I'd like the water rights."

"The river runs through the Dakotas, far north of us. You can't control all of it."

He smiled as if they were discussing the weather. She knew he expected her to jump at his spectacular offer. "No, I can't, but I'll feel better about it if I control more water than I do now. That's what our dads fought over. Plus, you have a thriving ranch. I would fully expect to make back my investment, or I wouldn't want it. There would be no point.

"I've made you a damn fine offer, Megan, and you know it. Think about it. Whatever you do about the ranch, I don't think you're going to spend a lot of your time in South Dakota."

"That's not the only consideration."

"You're hanging on out of anger, not because of a business decision. I know you don't run your gallery this way."

"I've never been emotionally involved with anyone the way I was with you, so it's difficult to view objectively," she admitted, hating to reveal the depth of her hurt. His eyes widened as if in disbelief, and she wondered what he was thinking about. Just being with him was opening doors to more problems and hurt. Thunder boomed again, as if a reminder to terminate the evening.

Staring at his supreme self-assurance in consternation, she knew he was right, but she wasn't going to let him win. "You're a ruthless man, Jared," she said flatly.

"No, I'm not. At least not in this case, and you know it. That's a fabulous bid, more than you'll get from anyone else. More than the place is worth. You've admitted that yourself. There's nothing ruthless about it. Most people wouldn't even be discussing the matter." He reached out to touch her hand, startling her and causing an unwelcome jump in her heartbeat. "But then, you're not 'most people,' and you never have been," he added in a husky voice that made her draw a deep breath. His gaze lowered to her mouth and her lips tingled. "You think about it," he suggested quietly, continuing to hold her hand. His hand slipped down to her wrist lightly, finding her racing pulse.

Satisfaction flared in his eyes, and she knew he could tell that she still had a strong physical reaction to him. The moment became taut, as his dark eyes probed hers. She should look away, move, speak—anything to end this electricity that intensified with each second; but she was held by his mesmerizing gaze. Memories rose to haunt her, tormenting moments of the past and their lovemaking. She could remember his kisses in exact detail, recollections she'd tried to shake.

"Stick to business," she said, the words bubbling up in anger even as her soft tone sheathed the steel in her voice.

She became aware of rain, wondering when it had begun, because she had been engrossed by their conversation. To her chagrin, she discovered it was a downpour, barely heard inside while sheets of water beat against the windows. She stood abruptly. "I'm going. I've stayed until it's pouring and I didn't intend to."

"Sit and wait it out," he suggested. "We can be civilized with each other. If you prefer, we can stay off the topic of business."

"The only thing I have to talk to you about, Jared, is business," she said, praying that was all she had to discuss with him and that he never learned the truth of why she was so unhappy to see him. The whole day and evening had turned into a nightmare, and she tried to hide her nervousness over seeing him again.

"You'll have a rough drive home. Let me take you and you can send a couple of your hands for your SUV tomorrow."

"No," she said, going to get her purse. Jared strolled behind her, his long legs eating up the distance with ease.

"Do you have a raincoat or umbrella?" he asked, and she shook her head.

"I didn't think about it. I have an umbrella in the SUV."

"I've got an extra. Wait a moment and I'll get it for you."

She watched him walk away, her gaze drifting over his long legs and through the memories of their bare strength against hers. Annoyed, she turned to the darkened window, watching rain beat against it. She wanted out of his house. Clearly, she recalled the muddy, rushing river nearly brushing Jared's bridge. She had to be able to get through. She couldn't stay the night with him.

To her relief, he reappeared with an umbrella and raincoat.

"Take both. I have others."

"Thanks. Where are you going?" she asked, as she watched him yank on a second raincoat.

"I'll follow you and see that you get across the

bridge. I intended to have it replaced, but I forget about it in the dry spells. We can go years without it being underwater."

"I can manage by myself. Thanks for dinner, Jared. I'll consider the offer and get back to you," she said over her shoulder, but he caught up with her, reaching ahead of her to open the door. His car was nowhere in sight, and she knew he would have to go back through the house or make a run for a garage. She didn't care what he did. Her focus was on crossing the river.

As she started the SUV and drove away, she peered through the watery windshield that couldn't be completely cleared by the wipers, even set on the highest speed.

Each flash of lightning increased her concern. Brilliant light illuminated fields that were turning into ponds, water running in the bar ditch. Occasionally, thin streams crossed low spots in the graveled road, and she knew the saturated ground was not soaking up the rain.

She couldn't be cut off. Not here and not now. Why had she let him goad her into this dinner? He would have made his pitch whether she showed up to eat with him or not.

Rounding a bend, she topped a rise when lightning flashed. She gasped as the streak of light revealed a river ahead. The instant display vanished, leaving driving rain and darkness, but the image was indelible in her mind. There was no bridge in sight because it was underwater.

She glanced in the rearview mirror and received another surprise. Headlights were a quarter of a mile

behind and gaining on her. It had to be Jared. How fast
was he driving in this storm?

She forgot about him as the next bolt lit up her surroundings, and again she saw the river with only the top
of the bridge rails showing.

With a sinking disappointment, she knew crossing
it would impossible. Jared pulled close behind, honked
his horn and stopped. He climbed out of his black
pickup, dashing to the passenger side of her SUV. Reluctantly, she unlocked the door to let him in out of the
storm.

"You can't cross the bridge. Sorry, Meg," he said as
he slid in, slamming the door.

"Megan!" she corrected. It was the first time he'd
called her Meg since he'd walked out on her.

"You'll have to come back to the house. I've got
plenty of room."

In another flash of lightning, she looked at the river
that spread out of its banks.

"I promise you this night will pass and be only a
memory," he said quietly, and she turned to find him
watching her. "If you'd like, I'll turn your SUV
around for you."

"Of course not, but thanks," she answered. "I've
gotten along on my own," she said, unable to keep her
resentment from showing.

Her cell phone rang, and she pulled it out of her
pocket and answered, only to hear her son's voice. She
glanced at Jared, fear and guilt returning as she said
hello to Ethan.

Jared waved at her and climbed out of the car.

Relieved to have him go, she let out her breath. A tense evening was now turning into a grim night. She talked briefly, promised she would call again when she was out of the storm. Then she turned her SUV around in water that lapped over new ground.

Still, the rain came in thick sheets, drumming on the SUV and shutting the world from view except what was caught in her twin headlights. Jared's pickup had faded from view quickly in the rain. The thought of being under the same roof with Jared through a stormy night frazzled her nerves. She didn't care how large his house was—it could never be big enough, being thrown together through the night and morning until the rain stopped.

She wasn't going to worry about tomorrow. Just get through tonight and resist his dark eyes. Their midnight depths held blazing desire, a continual hot-blooded look that made her tingle from head to toe. There was nothing circumspect, businesslike or remote about what she saw smoldering in his appreciative gaze.

When he was younger, he went after what he wanted with a single-mindedness that was fierce. She knew that intensity was focused on acquiring her ranch, but she didn't care to have it turned on seduction.

Squaring her shoulders, she promised herself to keep barriers between them and try to get him out of her life before he discovered what she never wanted him to know. The SUV slid on the wet road and she turned her full attention to driving.

As she expected, when she reached his house he was waiting on the lighted porch. He stood by the railing, one booted foot propped on the rail. If he

weren't so handsome and sexy, it would be far easier
to remain cool toward him. Too many shared moments
that, at the time, she had thought the best of her life,
made it impossible to deal with him objectively. She cut
the motor and sat a minute. The wind was blowing, a
thorough storm lashing the earth as if a mirror of her
emotions. Taking a deep breath, she stepped out with
the umbrella and dashed to the porch and into the house,
where she kicked off her impractical pumps. She left
her umbrella on the flagstone entryway. "I'll leave them
so I don't track water," she added, walking along the
wide hall with him, trying to block memories of being
in this house years ago. Her simmering anger crushed
conversation and she walked in silence.

"Remember any of this?" he asked.

"Of course," she answered in clipped tones, and he
glanced at her with his head tilted and one eyebrow
raised in a questioning glance that made her heart thud.
She knew that look only too well.

"You haven't changed much here, if my memory is
correct," she said, looking at potted palms and gilt-
framed seascapes.

"Not in this part of the house. I've left this part alone.
Otherwise, I had an addition built to the kitchen, as well
as a new bedroom for me. I'll show you later. How's
this room?" he asked, switching on a light and entering
a room with a king-size four-poster bed and maple furniture that stood on a polished oak floor.

"Fine," she said, following him into the room and
seeing the adjoining bathroom.

"Let's go back to the kitchen for something warm to

drink. What would you like—hot chocolate, hot tea or something cold?" he asked while they walked down the hall again.

"If you have some, I'd prefer hot tea," she answered. "I told my son I'd call him back. If you'll excuse me," she said, getting her cell phone from a pocket in her skirt. She went to the living area to stand at one of the floor-to-ceiling glass walls and watch the rain while she called Ethan. She missed him and just wanted to wrap her arms around him. Reassuring herself he was safe and happy with her relatives, she tried to quell her anxiety. Next she talked to her aunt to tell her she was marooned at Jared's ranch.

With each jagged streak of lightning, she saw that the drenching rain hadn't let up. The puddles had spread, increasing her concerns that she might be stranded in the morning.

Assuring her aunt she was fine, Megan put away her phone and rejoined Jared in the kitchen. Asking about his work, she perched on a bar stool and watched him set yellow china mugs on a large tray. Her gaze traveled over his features, so familiar to her. If he ever saw Ethan…

Her heart did a flip at the thought. With brown eyes and black hair, Ethan looked as much like his dad as a child could, even down to the cleft in his chin.

Another clap of thunder boomed and lights dimmed. Jared glanced toward the windows. "I'll get candles, in case," he said, crossing to disappear into a walk-in pantry.

"All I need," she mumbled softly, hoping she didn't

spend the evening in candlelight with him. He had too many things going for him already.

Still focusing conversation on his work, she followed him into the living area, where she curled up in a chair. Lights were low and Jared had switched on soft music, while rain still drummed outside and poured off the porch roof. He took the nearby sofa and placed a tray with their steaming cups of tea and coffee on the glass table in front of both of them. Usually, such surroundings would lend a cozy intimacy to the evening, but she planned to have her drink and get back to the bedroom and close the door on Jared for the night.

As he answered her inquiries about his Dallas and Paris offices, his traveling and his houses, she wondered if she had made the mistake of her life. Should she have revealed to Jared long ago that he was the father of her son?

Had she erred by never contacting Jared through the intervening years? The minute the question came, she knew if she had to do it all over again, she would do the same. Jared had walked out on her without a word, never contacting her until their encounter this morning.

The simmering resentment boiled momentarily as she remembered her joy and his declarations of love, the wild passion between them and then…desertion. He didn't contact her, give her any indication that anything was wrong—he left, and when she began to look for him, she discovered from his parents that he'd gone to Texas, where he'd taken a new job. They gave her his phone number, but she had no intention of calling him.

The hurt had been monumental, compounded when she'd learned she was pregnant.

To forgive and forget was impossible. Tonight, he wanted something from her, and therefore was flirting and charming once again; but there was a solid, lasting bedrock of pain that he'd caused.

Still, guilt nagged and worry plagued her. Had she cut her son out of a relationship that would have enriched his life? Yet, how could a man who left like that have been that role model? He might not have paid any attention to him, which would have multiplied hurts.

Again, she hated the painful memories—agonizing ones of Jared, hurtful moments with her father, who was enraged when he discovered her pregnancy. Jared had been gone two months by the time her father learned the truth, and from the first moment when the doctor had given her the news, she'd known that she would be alone when she had her baby.

It hadn't turned out that way, thanks to her aunt and uncle in Sioux Falls, who stood by her through Ethan's birth.

Jared tilted his head to give her another one of those quizzical looks that was so familiar. How often had she seen the same look from her son?

"I think I'm talking far too much about my life. Tell me about yours," Jared said. He sat back with one foot on his knee. A brilliant flash was followed by a window-rattling clap of thunder, and the lights dimmed and then went out.

"Sit tight," Jared said in the darkness. "We're ready for the emergency."

With the next flash of lightning, she saw him standing, holding a candle. He began to light candles and place them in holders on the table.

The hiss of rain could be heard clearly, since music no longer played. Candlelight flickered and bathed Jared in a golden glow, highlighting his prominent cheekbones, his thickly-lashed eyes, the cleft in his chin and the sheen in his well-trimmed black hair. Unbidden thoughts came, of running her hands through that thick hair which had a tendency to curl, particularly in damp weather. Most of the time, Jared fought the curls and kept them combed out as much as he could, taming them into slight waves. He sat again, closer to the end of the sofa and her chair. "You look gorgeous, especially in candlelight."

"Thank you," she answered, hating the stab of pleasure his compliment gave her. "In candlelight everyone looks appealing. And on another topic—do you work more in the U.S. or abroad?"

He looked amused as he answered. "A safer topic, as you wish. Far less interesting," he said. "I'm in the U.S. the majority of the time. Did you move to Santa Fe when you started making pottery?"

"Not right away," she answered. She couldn't imagine that he really cared what she'd done. "I worked for a decorator in Sioux Falls as well as on my own," she continued. "I marketed through a Web site, and through the decorator. I thought it would be good to work in Santa Fe, so I moved and eventually went out on my own."

"I doubt if your dad liked you leaving here."

"No, he didn't, but he decided it would be a good experience for me. I think he thought I'd fail and come home, despite the fact I'd even bought a house," she replied, remembering how frightening it had been to move and go on her own with a small son. She had worried about Ethan and if the change would hurt him. The early years she'd lived with constant worry.

"Did he ever recognize your talent?"

She smiled. "Once I began to make sufficient money, my dad's attitude changed."

"It usually does," Jared said. "Nothing succeeds like success. It's difficult to imagine you working in clay, though," he said, taking her hands in his warm ones. "These hands don't look like you're a potter."

He turned her hands in his, intensifying a smoldering desire that she couldn't extinguish with either anger or logic. Drawing a deep breath, she pulled her hands away.

"I liked holding your hands," Jared said in a husky voice.

"It's the storm and candlelight—and wine you had with dinner. I suspect you like holding the hand of almost any woman you spend the evening with."

He ran his finger along her cheek and studied her with a somber, intent look as he shook his head. "Perhaps, but this is different. I didn't know when I came back here and saw you that it would be this way."

Her heart drummed along with her annoyance at him. She had no intention of letting him rekindle an unwanted physical attraction. To her dismay, he still held appeal, but her emotions battled it.

Beyond her physical response to him, there was not only her smoldering rage over the hurt he'd inflicted by leaving but also icy fear over what he might discover about her now. To be in close proximity to him set her nerves on edge.

"Jared, this isn't a special moment, other than we may be having the rain of the year. Don't pour on the compliments because I have something you want. You have a captive audience tonight, but don't overdo it," she said, thankful she could sound detached. Anything to keep an emotional distance between them. Yet her heart raced and his words weren't going to be easily forgotten.

He gave her a crooked smile. "That wasn't the reason for the compliments, I promise you. Buying your ranch was the last thing on my mind," he added, in that same husky voice that was a caress in itself.

She finished her tea and stood. "I'll turn in. I rise early."

He stood. "It's early to turn in, Megan."

"Times change, Jared. We're different people. I'll take a candle." When she reached to pick up her dishes, his hand closed around her wrist. The touch was light and casual, but the outcome was an unwanted skip of her heartbeat. Warmth suffused her beyond anything the hot tea had accomplished. Startled, she glanced up.

"You know that's not true. Leave the dishes," he said, his husky voice revealing his reaction to the contact. She was bending over the table and he had leaned close to take her wrist. Now they were only inches apart, closer than before. Candlelight flickered with pinpoints of light reflected in his brown eyes.

Once again she was captive, as she'd been beneath his volatile kisses—those kisses that had always set her ablaze.

"Megan," he said softly.

"No," she answered with little force. A pang of yearning tore her, instantly followed by anger that he could still have such an impact on her. Worse, she knew he was on the verge of a kiss she very much wanted. "No," she repeated more firmly. She straightened and he dropped his hand, still watching her with searing fire in the depths of his eyes.

"We could declare a truce," he suggested softly. "That was long ago, Megan."

Holding back a seething retort, she glared at him. "This is a useless discussion," she said, hating that she couldn't appear more poised. Appear as if what he'd done years ago no longer mattered. She reached to light another candle, but he steadied her hand and they lit a candle together.

Once more, he was holding her wrist. His slight touch increased her awareness of him more. And he was taking his own sweet time getting the candle burning. She was tempted to yank away from his grasp, but she'd already been foolish enough to reveal how much she reacted to the past. Over the flickering light, she looked up to meet his hot gaze trained on her mouth. She couldn't get her breath. Her lips parted and she wanted him in spite of what was sensible.

"Light the candle, Jared," she whispered.

His thumb moved back and forth slowly, a feathery touch on her wrist, until he paused and she knew he

was fully aware that she always reacted to the slightest contact.

Desire magnified, pounding with each heartbeat.
Setting aside the candle, he slid his hand behind her head.

"Jared," she whispered, a protest that came out a
breathless invitation.

He drew her the last few inches and his mouth
covered hers.

His warm lips moved caressingly, his tongue
touching hers and then sliding deep into her mouth.
Longing, physical and emotional, tugged at her even as
she returned his passion. His other arm went around her
waist and he stepped around the corner of the table to
pull her body against his.

Once again, she was in his arms. How often had she
dreamed of this moment, only to wake and discover it
had been a fantasy. That Jared had still broken her heart
so ruthlessly. Amazingly, here she was, actually kissing
him, held in his strong embrace, finding him even sexier
than she'd remembered.

Heat became fire. She fought the urge to wind her
arms around him and press closer against him. Half of
her longed for him desperately and the other half
screamed to step away, to prevent what was happening.

His kisses burned wisdom to ashes. She kissed him
hungrily, aching for more, knowing she was tumbling
to disaster. Each second compounded her years-old
need. Finally, she pushed against his chest.

He released her slowly, opening his eyes to study her
in a heated silence.

"We're not going back there, Jared," she declared

with a gasp. "I didn't want that to happen. Don't make anything of it. It meant nothing, except I haven't kissed a man in a long time."

"Don't be so angry, Meg. I like kissing you," he said in a husky voice that held such warmth she tingled from head to toe. "No harm intended and no damage done," he added in unruffled assurance.

"Don't!" she cried. "I'm turning in," she said, circling the table in the opposite direction from Jared.

"You don't have to escort me to the bedroom door," she said, when he started toward her.

"Good night, Jared," she stated firmly.

"I wish I could take away your anger. We were young, Megan." His dark shirt was open at the throat and locks of hair had fallen over his forehead. Because of the rain, the natural curl in his hair had tightened and black curls framed his face.

She shook her head. "Good night," she repeated.

Emotionally exhausted, she entered her bedroom.

Her lips were still warm from his kisses and she was on fire with craving. The manner in which she had responded to him tore at her. He had opened Pandora's Box for her. She blamed it on not dating, but she kept busy and didn't miss having a man in her life. Between work and taking care of Ethan and his activities, her life was full, busy, so she fell exhausted into bed at night. But with a kiss, Jared had effortlessly demolished all her defenses. One touch, one kiss and she had been mush, melting and kissing him back. He'd made her yearn for his kisses and the feel of his warm, muscular body.

All yearnings she didn't want.

Crossing the room, she tried to forget that Jared was close, that he was soon to be undressed and stretched in bed. He used to sleep in the nude and she suspected he still did. Images plagued her, driving any chance of sleep away.

Why couldn't she have remained aloof and showed him that he couldn't stir her? Instead, she had responded passionately. She couldn't stop going over it, even though thinking about it made her hot. How could she have responded like that to a man whom she despised?

And his one million…

Sell him the ranch and she'd never see or hear from him again. Logic said to sell. She would get an incredible price, be rid of something she didn't care for anyway, She would sever most ties with South Dakota and only run a risk of seeing Jared when she visited her aunt and uncle. She would narrow the chances of Jared discovering what she had done.

On the other hand, she couldn't bear to deed the ranch to him. Fury over the hurts he'd inflicted tempted her to strike out at him in any way she could. Retribution was too enticing, something she had dreamed about for the first years after Jared's disappearance.

Plus, her father would never sell Jared the ranch. Her dad had hated the Daltons, despising Jared's father because of their continual fights over water. Each one had accused the other of taking too much. Water fights had always spilled over into every other contact. If a fence went down, each man blamed the other.

She knew, too, her father had viewed Jared's dad's simple background with disdain, as if he were a peasant. When Jared had walked out on her, her father had hated him for hurting her, even though he had been doing his best to talk her out of marrying Jared when Jared had vanished. Many issues fueled the family feud.

Both sides of her argument were strong. Money versus emotional satisfaction.

When her father's health began to fail, he had deeded the ranch to her. Upon his death, that decision became a safety net for her. It saved her time and money to have the ranch already in her possession, and left her free to sell it.

Each time she thought about Jared walking out on her and now coming back to buy the ranch, she felt as if she couldn't bear to sell—at any price.

Was she harming herself and Ethan by her refusal to let Jared buy the ranch? The money would be more than enough to provide for Ethan's education and a comfortable lifestyle they could never have otherwise. If she refused Jared, she might not get anywhere near her asking price from other buyers.

She was certain she would sell, but it could take a while—time she really didn't want to devote to the care of the ranch. It took money to keep it running smoothly, and with her father's failing health the past year, there were areas that had been neglected. The sensible business and professional approach was to sell to Jared or counter for an even higher amount—something she suspected he would agree to, to get what he wanted.

She knew she would pore over the arguments all night long. So far, the only person interested in the ranch had been Jared. She curled up in a chair near the window, watching the rain and flashes of lightning. Hopefully, once the rain stopped, the river would drop rapidly.

She rubbed her temples. Sleep would likely elude her for hours. To sell or not to sell? Stop remembering his touch and being aggravated with herself for succumbing to his slightest touch.

She paced to the window to stare outside, blowing out the candle to depend on lightning flashes for illumination.

If she would agree to sell the ranch, it would be the quickest way to get Jared out of her life. She stood at the window watching rivulets of water zigzag their way along the glass. Flashes of lightning revealed small rivers running through the yard and large silver puddles. The river would be high and impossible to cross, and the rain hadn't slacked off any.

She returned to a chair to stare outside while her thoughts churned over her predicament. Far into the night, she fell asleep in the chair.

Dawn was streaked with rays of the rising sun, lifting her spirits and giving her hope that she could leave soon.

She still struggled with her decision. Because of her fury at Jared, and her father's memory, she didn't want to sell. Keeping the ranch when Jared wanted it would give her immense satisfaction and a bit of revenge.

At the same time, the argument to sell couldn't be dismissed lightly.

She fell asleep in the chair, and woke undecided in the morning. Gathering her things, she headed to the bathroom to shower and dress in what she had worn the evening before. After combing her hair, she went to the kitchen, where she found Jared with a cup of coffee on the table in front of him. Dressed in jeans and a short-sleeved, gray Western shirt and boots, he looked irresistible.

"Good morning," he said easily, walking over to her, his gaze roaming over her appreciatively. "You're gorgeous—as you were last night," he said, curling a lock of her hair around his fingers. "This is the way I like your hair best." Catching the scent of his masculine aftershave, she felt her pulse kick up.

"Thank you for your compliment," she replied, wishing she had done something else with her hair. She didn't care to wear it in the style he liked best. "I'm a little overdressed for breakfast, but so be it."

"I could loan you my jeans," he said, with a twinkle in his eyes.

"No, thanks," she answered quickly.

"I didn't think you'd accept, but they wouldn't fit you anyway. I cooked breakfast—help yourself to whatever you like," he said, waving his hand toward covered dishes and pans on a stove. "Fruit is on the table. Would you like orange juice or tomato juice, milk, coffee—you can have all if you'd like."

"Orange juice and coffee please," she said, picking up a plate and looking at the many dishes. She helped herself to scrambled eggs, slices of kiwi and a bowl of blackberries. She had lost her appetite. As she watched him serve her juice and coffee, she knew she couldn't bear to sell him the ranch, no matter how much refusing him cost her. She would get a bit of satisfying retaliation here.

"This is a huge breakfast. Do you cook often?"

"Not unless there's no alternative. This morning we're cut off from my kitchen help."

"Looks like I'm here longer." She carried her plate to the table where he sat facing her.

"There are all sorts of things we could do to fill the day," he stated, causing her to look up sharply. When he gave her a disarming smile, she shook her head, smiling in return.

"I think simple conversation is the most likely. Or if you have business you can transact, you go right ahead."

"I wouldn't dream of it. If you don't sell your ranch to me, we'll be neighbors, so we might as well get reacquainted."

"I see no point in that," she said quickly.

"You surely don't plan for us to go through the future fighting, the way our fathers did."

"No...but reacquainted—I don't think so."

"So what's it going to be? To sell or not to sell?" he asked.

Three

Jared's pulse drummed as she faced him. Intuition hinted she would refuse him. Using logic, he couldn't imagine her rejecting his money.

"You made me a generous offer. One that kept me up almost all night," she said.

"A shame. I can think of other ways we could have spent the time," he said, unable to avoid flirting in spite of the tension between them. She was breathtaking, and he wanted to reach for her. Sunlight spilled through the windows and highlighted strands in her cascade of black hair. Her eyelashes were a thick, dark fringe that were a startling contrast with the crystal turquoise of her eyes. He waited in silence until she shook her head, dismissing his remark.

"I won't sell the Sorenson ranch to you," she answered.

His insides knotted and he curbed the urge to swear, instead remaining impassive, smiling at her as he shrugged. "That's what you want to do. You're turning down an extra one million."

"You received that well, Jared. Too well. I pulled the ranch off the market and decided to keep it."

"Even with your son to consider?"

Her face flushed and something flickered in her eyes and he knew he'd hit a nerve. "Yes, Ethan and I will get along without your money. We have thus far."

He was disappointed, but the world held countless opportunities. "Win some, lose some," he repeated the old saying. "Maybe you'll change your mind about selling after you spend a few years going back and forth and maintaining the ranch and your Santa Fe home."

"I'll manage, Jared."

"Well, I'm disappointed, but if you're not going to sell to me and go hurrying back to New Mexico," he said, approaching, "there's a bright side." He placed his hands on her shoulders, sliding one hand under the large bow that fastened her dress over her shoulder. "We'll be neighbors," he said in a warm voice. Undeniably, he wanted her more than her ranch. "You'll have to come home more often… I'll certainly spend more time here."

Drawing a deep breath, she frowned. "We'll be neighbors, not *seeing* each other."

"You opposed anything concerning me, Meg," he said in a husky voice. "We're bound to see each other, and why not? Why cling to the past? I told you I was sorry. Your refusal to sell guarantees I'll be around," he said.

"That wasn't my intention," she said. Her words were unfriendly but her tone wasn't. Her protests were light, almost halting, and contradictory to what she was saying—an unspoken invitation to him. "Not at all, Jared."

"Well, that's the result you've achieved. You've put me back into your life. I'm looking forward to being your neighbor."

"Go back to Texas, Jared. You know this is going nowhere."

"If you really want me out of your life so badly, maybe you should think some more about this answer you've given me. I can't help but feel that there's some part of you that wants to keep me here."

She twisted out of his grasp as his cell phone rang. He took it out of his pocket. "Excuse me, Megan," he said, answering his phone and talking briefly.

"That was one of the hands," he said when he was finished. "The river is still as the bridge level—some water washing over, but you can get through."

"Great!" she cried. "I'm going home."

She was clearly combating the physical attraction with all her being, a battle he felt she would eventually lose. He knew how to be patient, and the bet had been the most exciting thing he had going. Until she came along.

"I'll go first, Megan," he said as they walked to the door. He took a wide-brimmed, black Stetson off a hat rack and put it on. They stepped out into warm sunshine and a day that was crisp and clear, with a deep blue sky. A vast difference from the stormy night.

At her SUV door, he paused. "Wait and let me go ahead. I'll cross the bridge to make sure it'll hold. After I get to the other side, you can cross."

"I know I'm wasting my breath when I say you don't have to accompany me."

"Stop cutting off your nose to spite your pretty face, Megan."

"I'll try, Jared," she said with sarcasm lacing her voice.

"Keep your SUV doors unlocked so you can get out or I can get in to help you. Let me clear the bridge before you follow. If it shifts or anything indicates it's weakened, I won't motion to you to proceed. Okay?"

"Yes, thanks. I'll follow you."

"Megan," he said in a deep voice, "I'm glad you were here last night. It's good to see you and be with you again. Better than ever," he said, thinking about their kisses and her eager response. If she reacted that much in anger, what would it be like if he could melt those hurdles she kept between them?

"It was meaningless, Jared. The result of my not dating enough and a turbulent night. And you know you hold a certain charm for me, whether I like it or not."

"I think there may have been a left-handed compliment somewhere in there. I certainly hope so," he said.

She shook her head and he held the door, assessing her long, shapely legs as she climbed into the SUV. He closed her door and hurried to his pickup. As he got in he caught her watching him. Once again, he had the feeling that he was missing something with her and he couldn't fathom what.

* * *

Passing her, he worried about the safety of the bridge.

He topped the rise and looked at the muddy, rushing water that was tumbling and flowing as rapidly as the night before, sending rivulets over the bridge. It was standing, but the force of the water could have taken a big toll on it. He slowed and saw she was only a short distance behind him. Stopping, she waited while he proceeded.

As soon as they had crossed, he stopped and walked over to talk to her through her open window. Leaning closer, he pushed his hat to the back of his head. "Would you like to go to dinner tonight?"

She shook her head. "No, Jared. Business between us is finished. There's no reason for us to get together again. I meant no sale. And it's good-bye."

He slid his hand behind her head, leaned down and kissed her hard, thrusting his tongue into her mouth, aware of her soft hair tangled in his fingers and spilling over his hand.

He'd caught her by surprise, but she kissed him back, arousing him instantly. He was tempted to open the SUV door, slide inside and take things further, but he knew that would end the kiss.

She pulled away. She was breathless, her eyes filled with longing, her mouth red from his kiss. "Good-bye, Jared," she whispered, but her inviting expression contradicted the farewell.

He stepped back. "Call if you change your mind. Otherwise, I'll see you soon," he said, knowing he was annoying her.

Without a word she drove away and he watched, standing in the road with his hands on his hips, until her beige SUV disappeared from sight.

She was more beautiful than when she'd been eighteen. More poised, infinitely more sexy. He wanted her and didn't intend for her to go out of his life until he had seduced her.

He suspected that might take awhile, but he wasn't a marrying man and he wasn't the green twenty-four-year-old that he had been.

And he still expected to buy her ranch. It would be ridiculous to refuse to sell to him because of old hurts. He didn't see how she could possibly mean no.

He climbed into his pickup to cross the river and drive back to the house, lost in thoughts about Megan, about making love to her when she'd been eighteen, naked and passionate. He stirred uncomfortably. He wanted her in his arms in his bed. With a groan he tried to get the erotic images out of mind.

If he could get past her smoldering anger, she could be seduced. Even as she burned with indignation, she hadn't rejected his touch and his kisses. Attraction was still alive between them. It was only a matter of time, he felt certain, until seduction. Everything in her cried out to him.

The future didn't hinge on Megan selling the ranch to him. He could move on to the next lucrative deal. This had looked like an easy one that could have been handled quickly, made him some easy money and cinched the bet.

A jingle interrupted his thoughts. He answered his cell phone again, to hear his cousin's voice.

"Hey, Matt here. Chase said you're in South Dakota. I wanted to see if you've been washed away. The rain is making national news."

"Thanks for call," Jared replied. "I'm fine. Bridge was underwater last night, but we have sunshine today and the water's receded."

"That's good news. I hear you're buying the Sorenson place—that's sweet payback!"

"The old man died, but it's still sweet payback with Megan," Jared said, thinking about her refusal and feeling certain he'd get his way eventually.

"Good luck with it. It doesn't matter, though, I still intend to win our bet."

"Wishful thinking. Thanks for your call," Jared said, smiling and remembering a pugnacious look Matt often had when he wanted something that was difficult to acquire. Beneath the curly black hair was a brain that clicked constantly.

"Go back to work. You'll need to do all you can," Matt teased, and was gone. Jared chuckled over the good-natured teasing and the competitiveness that had been present since as far back as he could remember. He glanced at his calendar, Matt's call fading from his attention.

Monday morning, he was scheduled to see his attorney in Sioux Falls before he headed home to Dallas and now he had a lunch appointment with his real estate agent. As Megan invaded his thoughts again, he forgot about a schedule.

Monday, the eighth of June, he dressed in a charcoal

suit and tie and drove himself, leaving behind his bodyguard and chauffeur, feeling secure in South Dakota.

In Sioux Falls, he drove downtown to his attorney's office. It was another sunny June day.

As soon as lunch was finished, he parted with the real estate agent and headed to his car, his thoughts already turning from South Dakota, as he mentally ran through projects for the week. He paused to call his pilot to be certain his plane would be ready. As he talked, he glanced up the wide main street and saw an unmistakable dark head of hair.

His pulse speeded—it had to be Megan. She stood in front of a restaurant talking to two people with a boy beside her. He had his back to Jared and wore a ball cap.

Jared recognized her aunt and uncle and guessed that Megan had her son with her.

Impulsively, he crossed the street in long strides. Megan was dressed in red slacks and a red, short-sleeved cotton shirt and her back was to him. Her hair was caught up in a clip high on her head.

It had been years since he had seen Olga or Thomas Sorenson, the older half-brother of Megan's father, Edlund.

"Hello, there, Megan," he said cheerfully. They all turned to face him, and once again Megan's face drained of color.

"It's been years," he said, extending a hand to Thomas Sorenson, who hesitated a few seconds and then reached out. In that first moment, her uncle and aunt had looked as shaken as Megan.

Under Thomas's solemn, half-angry gaze, Jared realized something was amiss. Tall and graying, Thomas Sorenson gave him the barest possible handshake. Jared smiled at Olga Sorenson, Thomas's diminutive blond wife, who merely nodded with tight lips. His sudden departure seven years ago resonated badly with all three adults even today. Jared turned to Megan who was frowning at him.

"Sorry, if I interrupted you folks, but I saw you and thought I'd say hello. I didn't intend to intrude," he said.

When his pleasant comment was met by awkward silence, his curiosity grew. He glanced at the boy, who was looking at a bright red toy rocket he held in his hands. "This must be your son, Ethan," Jared said, holding out his hand in greeting. "Ethan, I'm Jared Dalton."

The boy looked up and shook hands with Jared.

"I'm glad to—" Jared's words died, as if he had been punched in the stomach. With midnight eyes, a cleft in his chin and black curls escaping from his cap, the boy staring back at him was his own image, a face that would match childhood pictures of Jared himself.

His own son!

Four

Jared glanced at Megan and her expression confirmed that Ethan Sorenson was his son. For an instant, he forgot the others as Megan's terrified gaze captured his. Her wide-eyed mixture of fear and anger put all the reactions this past weekend in place for him.

The moment would become permanently etched in Jared's memory—sun shining brightly, the three adults facing him with a mixture of unfriendliness and guilt in their expressions. And Ethan, who was looking at his rocket once more and unaware of the undercurrents.

The boy seemed not to have recognized Jared. All these years, Jared had had a son. The enormity of it overwhelmed him and for a moment he was at a loss. Megan had never told him. By all indications, she wasn't going to tell him now, either. She had been planning to let him go back to Texas without ever knowing about his son.

Astounded over his discovery and her duplicity, his gaze shifted from Ethan to her.

"I need to see you," he said to Megan. "We have to talk now."

She nodded and turned to tell Ethan good-bye and hug him.

"It was nice to see you," he said to the Sorensons. "Ethan, I'm glad to meet you," he said.

His *son!* When would he grow accustomed to that? He longed to pull the child into his arms and just hold him for a minute. Instead, he smiled.

"How old are you, Ethan?" he asked.

"Six, sir," Ethan answered politely, an unnecessary confirmation. Jared had left seven years ago and Ethan must have been born nine months later.

The Sorensons bade Ethan come with them and they strolled away.

Jared thought about where they could get some privacy as quickly as possible. He wasn't waiting to drive out to her ranch or his own to talk. Questions spun, anger was like wildfire consuming him.

Why hadn't his staff unearthed the parentage of her child? The marriage. A marriage on the rebound—or to give an excuse for the pregnancy?

"They know the truth, don't they?" he asked Megan.

"Yes, they do. I'm close to them, closer than I was to my dad," she said.

Jared placed his hand on her arm. "We can't discuss

this on the street. Let's go to the hotel and I'll get us a room where we can have privacy."

"Hotel? We can go to the ranch."

"No," he said flatly. "I'm not waiting through a long drive. I have questions, Megan, and I want answers now." In the taut silence, she gave him a stormy look; the clash of wills crackled between them.

As she clamped her mouth closed, he escorted to the tall, remodeled hotel.

She slanted him a look. "I thought you were leaving town today."

"I had planned to fly out at one," he said, and she turned away while he left her to step to the desk to get them a suite.

In silence they rode the elevator to the fifth floor, where they entered a large suite decorated in muted earth tones of umber and green and deep red. Sunshine poured through floor-to-ceiling glass windows and doors, giving a sunny glow to the room and sharply contrasting Jared's icy rage.

She crossed the sitting room, putting distance between them before she turned to glare at him defiantly. "You walked out, Jared. You have no claim. Absolutely none."

"The hell I don't!" he snapped, shedding his coat to drop it on a chair. "That's my son. Why didn't you call me?"

"Call you?" she raised her voice, her cheeks flushing a deep pink, shaking with anger. She leaned forward. "Why would I call you when it was obvious that you never wanted to see me again?"

He crossed the room to clasp her shoulders. "You should've let me know that I was going to be a father. You damn well know it," he said, grinding out the words, shaking himself.

"Get your hands off me!" she ordered, jerking away from him. "You asked for whatever happened."

"Is that why you married, or did you have some kind of rebound relationship?"

She looked away and bit her lip before turning back to him. "The marriage was solely because I was pregnant."

"You were never in love?" he asked in surprise, feeling glad even through his rage. "You didn't marry to get even? Wasn't that guy furious when he discovered what you'd—"

"No, he wasn't, because our marriage was a business arrangement. My father negotiated it to cover up the paternity of my baby!" She flung the words at him.

"Negotiated?" Jared asked in disbelief. "You went along with that?"

"Damn you, Jared! You crushed me and left me and I was pregnant. My control freak father was enraged. He said horrible things. Then he contracted for the marriage and it was all settled beforehand."

His anger toward her father returned full force. How the bastard tried to govern everything. "Your meddling father—what did he do exactly?" Jared asked, unable to stop prying, yet knowing he was going to hate what he would hear.

"He arranged or, rather, bought my marriage," she said, pronouncing the words slowly and distinctly as if Jared were unfamiliar with English.

"Where did he find the guy?" Jared asked while his hurt multiplied.

"Mike was the son of a Montana rancher. By then, he was an engineer, living in Phoenix. My father paid him to marry me."

"And you went along with that?"

"What was I supposed to do? It was a paper marriage, a business arrangement to give the baby a father."

"He wasn't our baby's father. Did you even live under the same roof?"

"For a little over a month. The marriage was never consummated. We had separate bedrooms and each of us went our own way. Mike had no interest in me. He only wanted the money to open his own firm. But under that guise of respectability, my father would pay for the baby and my care."

"That bastard!" Jared exclaimed, rage eating at him. He had thought when he'd left South Dakota that the Sorensons could never hurt him again. How wrong he'd been! To discover she'd hidden the most important thing in his life from him—his son—cut to his soul.

"Who are you to say that?" she answered. "You walked out and left me pregnant! Damn you, Jared! I was uneducated, young and dependent on my dad."

It was on the tip of his tongue to reveal her father's duplicity, but he wasn't going to get into that now, or hurling accusations would be all they would do. He wanted to know about Ethan.

"So go on—tell me what you did. You married Mike and moved to Arizona."

"That's right. Under the circumstances, I was less than pleasant. Mike was interested in his career and I think there was someone in his life, but he was kind enough to keep her out of our lives. We got a quiet divorce after seven weeks and I left."

"You came home once for a reception, I heard."

"Yes, so Dad could convince people that Ethan was Mike's son."

"How could anybody believe that lie after Ethan was born?"

She shrugged. "I don't know what gossip flew, nor did I care by then."

"I got a degree of revenge on your father in Ethan, since he looks exactly like me. Your father had to be constantly reminded of me," Jared said. No one who knew both him and Ethan could mistake the connection. "Do you ever see Mike?"

"No. We went our separate ways and I haven't talked to him since," she said, and Jared was surprised by the relief he experienced over her answer. "My dad used to tell me about him occasionally. I think he'd even hoped we'd stay married. Mike established his own firm and married. That's the last I heard about him."

"Damn it," Jared said. All they had both gone through because of her father. "And in all that time, it didn't occur to you to let the father of your baby know about his son's existence?"

"Don't, Jared! Don't accuse me—"

He grasped her shoulders again, fighting the urge to shake her. "I'm the father, and in this day and age I have rights. Yes, I accuse you. You know damned well you should've let me know we were having a baby."

"I never once when I was pregnant thought I should let you know," she said, the words tumbling out in a rage.

"When I first spoke to you last Saturday, you went white as a sheet and looked as if you might faint." His voice was low, and he leaned closer with anger white hot. "You were filled with guilt for keeping silent. Admit it, Megan! Admit that you know you should've told me about Ethan."

Her eyes were wide and green with anger as she shook her head, adding to his fury. "No. You gave that right up when you walked out without a word. You cut all ties with me in the cruelest possible way."

When he flinched because what she accused him of was true, he still couldn't bring himself to reveal to her that it was her father, because it would sound weak, as if he were making excuses. "Maybe I deserved for you to keep me out of your life, but when Ethan was born, you know you should have informed me. If you'd told me you were expecting a baby, I would've come back here."

"Oh, please, Jared! Don't stretch credulity to that point! You know you wouldn't have. You would have run all the more, if I'd called you and said you were about to become a father. Or you would've asked if I was sure it was your child."

"That's not true," he said in a voice that was low and vehement. "I damn well would've come back."

"You'll never, ever convince me of that. It's a moot point now," she said, glaring at him and he noticed she was breathing as rapidly as he was.

"Even so, I can't believe that in all these years you haven't told me. I can't understand why my own parents didn't tell me, but they moved from here two years later."

"I didn't see your parents. I didn't come home to live for a year and a half. People here met Mike at the reception, so they accepted the story that he was the father. Your parents moved shortly after I returned."

"I still say you should have told me. You know you should have. When you moved back here, you could have faced dealing with letting me know. We'd put enough time between us—"

"Enough time between us that I no longer hurt from what you did?" she flung the words at him as he clamped his jaw closed while he clenched his fists.

"Even so—"

"All right," she said, her voice suddenly sounding restrained. "When Ethan was one, I should've informed you. But I always thought I would when he got a little older, or if you came home and we crossed paths. Or if you tried to contact me, which of course, you didn't until you wanted something I have. Whenever a year rolled by, I put off telling you again." His anger was mirrored in the depths of her eyes. "What was I to do? Pick up the phone and call the man who walked out on me and say, 'Oh, by the way, we had a baby'? You left without a word—that means you wanted to sever all ties with me. Why on earth would I call you?" she cried. "Can't you get it?"

"I deserved to know, Megan, simply because I'm his father," Jared said. "I guess you don't know a parent's rights, but I do have rights. Where was Ethan born?"

"In Chicago, where we had gone to college. It's a large city and far from here."

Jared's pain over the past intensified. "You were alone in Chicago? Did you have any friends?"

"I'm sure you care!" she exclaimed bitterly. "Jared, this is all past."

"I want to know what happened. Answer my damn questions."

"If you must know, my aunt came to stay with me the last two weeks. My dad never came. After Ethan was six months old, he told me to come back home."

"Well, I got some damned revenge there. Ethan looks like me. What a blow that must have been."

"It was to all of us. I prayed he wouldn't look like you—and that you'd never know," she said, the coldness and anger clear in her voice.

"Damn it, Megan!"

"Damn it is right! I prayed my baby wouldn't resemble you in any way and that you'd never know as long as you lived. How can you act like you care now?"

"It's a shock to discover I have a child. I have questions. And frankly, Megan, I want to know my son."

She looked as if he'd hit her. And then he could see her pull herself together in that manner she had. She stood taller, a coolness coming to her features.

"Was it difficult for you when you came back home? With one look at Ethan, I'd think anyone would've known who his father was."

"How much gossip there was, I don't know," she admitted. "In the course of months, other scandalous things happened around this area, so interest shifted. It didn't matter after we moved to Santa Fe and it never has again, I'm sure you and I were a major source of gossip until I married Mike. You couldn't tell who Ethan's dad was by looking, until after the boy got a full head of hair. While he was a baby, people thought that he was Mike's child. Dad was smart enough to find a guy who bore a physical resemblance to you—black hair, dark brown eyes, tall. It was inevitable that Ethan would have black hair. No one would give that a thought."

"I'll bet my folks never laid eyes on him. One look at him, hair or no hair, and my mom would've known."

"As a matter of fact, they didn't."

"Damn it, even if I did walk without telling you good-bye, you should've let me know about our baby. I know now, though," he said coldly. "We're going to have to work something out," he said.

She walked away to stand by the floor-to-ceiling glass door before she turned back to face him. "You keep your distance. You forfeited all rights to Ethan when you walked out on me. You're not coming into our lives now, Jared. Forget that one. I don't see that you have any rights in the matter."

"I damn well do. You're not going to pack and go and take him away from me."

"I'm going home. You know what happened after you left me, and this is getting us nowhere."

"How the hell can you walk out of here and try and say good-bye? Understand me, Megan, I intend to get to know my son," he declared, his temper rising. He clenched his fists and inhaled deeply.

He stood with his hands on his hips and they glared

at each other, the clash fierce between them. In spite of
all his fury, he wanted her. She was as beautiful and
enticing as she was infuriating. Long strands of her
black hair had come loose from the clip and fell around
her face. Her cheeks were flushed and her eyes wide,
and she was enticing in spite of the struggle between
them. He desired her and he wished she would cooperate with him—both impossibilities.

"All right, we'll go back to the ranch and discuss it,"
he said. "You come to my place or I'll go to yours. The
sun is shining, no rain is predicted and the river has
lowered enough that the bridge is definitely above water."

"I see no point in arguing further," she said.

"Megan, I will get to know Ethan. That's a fact, not
a wish," he stated, trying to control his temper, pushed
to his limit. "We can discuss what we're going to do in
the future. Your ranch or mine will be more comfortable for both of us and this may take a while."

She clamped her lips closed for a moment. "I know
you've had a shock. The drive to the ranch will give you
some time to adjust to your new status and to think
about all that's happened. Don't tear up Ethan's life.
You think about it when you drive home. You're being
selfish again. I know you're accustomed to thinking
only of yourself, but you'll hurt him if you come into
his life. And you'll raise a hundred questions."

"You should have thought of those questions," Jared
said. "You should have known that this day would come."

"It wouldn't have happened if you hadn't wanted to
buy the ranch," she said bitterly.

"You might have slipped by if you'd sold it to me.

My attorneys would have handled the deal, and I doubt if you and I would have crossed paths except at the closing, and then you would have left for New Mexico and I would've gone on my way. Big error, Megan, if you'd really hoped to keep me from Ethan."

Her face flushed and he knew he'd been correct in all he'd stated.

"Perhaps, but I couldn't bear the thought of selling to you. You get what you want in life too easily."

"Well, now you pay the price for that refusal."

Frowning, she picked up her purse and hurried to the door. "If you insist, I'll see you at my ranch. I'm not taking any chance of getting marooned at yours again."

Grabbing his coat, he caught up to hold the door and walk out with her. "We'll start another flurry of rumors by this little interlude in the hotel."

"I can't worry about that. I don't plan to live here," she said. "I don't have many close friends here any longer. The few that I have are close enough to understand and to know that there will never be anything between you and me again."

"You can't foretell the future," he said.

"I can predict that much with certainty. There's too much bitterness on either side for it to vanish."

He didn't answer, his mind reeling with his discovery and what he'd learned from her. He escorted her to the street where she motioned with her hand. "My car is parked right there. I'll see you at home."

"All right. This will give you time to think, too."

She nodded and walked quickly away. His gaze traveled over her, looking at the sway of her hips and her leggy stride while he thought about their future. He hurried to his car and in minutes he was out of town.

As he drove to the ranch, he pored over their conversation. His mind kept going back to that startling moment when Ethan looked up at him. Jared vowed that he wasn't going to be out of Ethan's life. Megan wasn't thinking straight, and he knew he had rights. He'd heard too much about a birth father's rights. He'd never let her cut him out of Ethan's life now.

Damn her bastard father. Now Jared could understand her bitterness and anger. Why hadn't she called and let him know? No undoing the past now—but he wasn't leaving here without settling up when and how he could have Ethan with him and be talking to Ethan as his father.

Now he could understand her frightened and unhappy aunt and uncle's reactions. Only Ethan was oblivious to the emotional tempest swirling around him.

Realizing how fast he was driving, Jared eased his foot and set cruise control while his mind was still on Ethan. All the years of Ethan's life he had missed, babyhood, toddler—it hurt, and he vowed that this distance was going to end as soon as possible.

He tried to think of ways they could share Ethan's life. They needed solutions, not accusations and anger. How could they work it out to share their child, when they had such disparate lives, and while she was so furious with him?

In front of Megan's ranch house, he spotted her car outside her garage. As he crossed the porch, she opened the door. "Come in, Jared," she said.

He entered a wide hallway that he hadn't seen for the past seven years, recalling the last time he'd walked along the hall and out the front door. He'd been hurt, his life had changed and he wouldn't see Megan again—until this year. All because of her father.

He followed her into a spacious living area that was just as he remembered, with a huge stone fireplace, animal head trophies on the walls, a large gilt-framed portrait of her father, Edlund, on one wall and a smaller picture of Megan beside it. Leather-covered furniture filled the room, along with a wide-screen television and ceiling fans that slowly turned overhead. The polished wood floor held Navajo rugs. Window shutters were open. Memories crowded him—some not good.

She turned to face him. "Let's get this over with. I hope you've done some thinking and that you've calmed. Jared, your life is too busy to give much attention to a child."

"Your life isn't busy?" he asked with cynicism.

"Of course it is. But I don't travel the world or have much social life or have any lifestyle like you do, and my kiln and studio are at home, and my gallery is attached to the house, so I can be with him when he's home."

"I'm glad to hear that."

"Oh, please!" she replied. "You have an interest in him because of the novelty of discovering you're related to him."

His anger climbed. "Megan, I want my son part of the time, and I'm going to have him. Now, what can we work out?"

Frowning, she shook her head. "I can't think of any feasible plan. You live and have your headquarters in Dallas. You travel the world. I reside and work in New Mexico and here. That makes it impossible for him to see you often."

Jared clamped his mouth shut and jammed his hands into his pockets, turning to walk to the window and gaze outside while he mulled over possibilities of what they could do.

"I don't see any hope for this, and I worry that you're going to upset his life," she said.

Jared whirled around. "I'm his *father!* If you'd told me, I'd have been in his life from the day he was born. If I upset his life, it will be only initially. Kids adjust. I expect to win him over, Megan. Can't you see that it will be good for him to have a father around?"

She turned away, but he'd seen her frown and her teeth catch her lower lip. He walked up behind her and tried to speak quietly. "It'll be better for him to have a dad who's interested in him. There are things I can do with him that you can't. Stop depriving him of a father."

"Don't act like I'm hurting him by keeping you out of his life!" she snapped, whirling around to face him, tears in her eyes.

"Megan," he said, grasping her shoulders gently.

She twisted free and walked away from him. "Don't, Jared!"

"We were in love seven years ago," he said quietly, following her to stand close behind her. "We both were present when Ethan was conceived. I was in that bedroom, too."

She turned again to face him, green fire flashing in her eyes. "Next, you'll be telling me you love me," she said.

"No," he admitted, placing his hands on her upper arms and rubbing them lightly. "But I know we can be compatible, we have been, and we have some kind of electricity between us. You can't deny it. I think you and I can find a common ground once more," he said, trailing his fingers lightly along her soft cheek. "Our lives became irrevocably bound with Ethan's birth, so let's put our heads together and see what solutions we can find."

"That's because you're the one searching for the answer to your dilemma," she said, glaring at him.

He was tempted to kiss away some of her stubborn refusal. Her passionate response earlier seemed to let all her barricades crumble. His gaze went to her mouth and he battled the urge to kiss her and stop the arguing.

As if she sensed his intentions, she walked farther from him.

"One way or another, Megan, we're going to work this out," he said.

She turned to perch on the edge of a leather wingback chair. He sat in another, facing her. "I thought of several things when I was driving here."

"I can well imagine," she remarked dryly.

Annoyed with her steady refusal to cooperate with him, he tried to hang on to his tattered patience. He was unaccustomed to people saying no to him, unaccustomed to a woman being so unyielding with him. Knowing he had to work this out with her, he sat back in his chair and took a deep breath. "A large percentage of problems have solutions if people pursue finding them," he said. "And *want* to find them," he added. Megan wanted him out of her life and that of his son, but that wasn't going to happen. There was no way he would stay out of Ethan's life now.

"Have you even tried to think what might work out?" he asked.

"Frankly, no, because nothing would."

He considered the possibilities he'd mulled over in the car while driving to the ranch. "Fine. You have him during the school year. I get him for most of the summer."

"No! He spends one month with my aunt and uncle, who are like grandparents to him."

"He can do that, and I get him the other months and during spring break."

"I won't do it, Jared. Ethan's been so close with me. The first years of his life, I was home with him constantly. It's just the two of us. He won't want to go off next summer for two months and live with you." She crossed her long legs.

"Not next summer, *this* summer," Jared corrected emphatically, and she shook her head.

"I don't want to share Ethan with you."

"You're going to," he said lightly, knowing he would never give up. He felt certain the law would be on his side. Her stubbornness was driving his anger, and he tried to calm down and think of what they could do that would be acceptable to both.

"Here's another idea, Megan. See if this is palatable. A marriage of convenience."

Five

"A marriage of convenience. You've already had one before," Jared said, and Megan's temper shot up.

"You're only after Ethan to get my ranch," she replied. "A marriage of convenience or any other kind would give you access to the ranch." She shook her head. "Never!"

He stood and approached her, stopping only yards from her, his brown eyes harboring anger that buffeted her in waves. She raised her chin to meet his gaze.

"I'm not doing any of this to get your damned ranch!" he declared gruffly, and she knew he was fighting to hang on to his temper as much as she was. "I want my son!" he said. "Can't you understand that?"

"Frankly, no! You don't strike me as the daddy type. Not at all. You're a well-known society playboy, a jet-setter, and I think you want Ethan to help get you access to my ranch, either because of the novelty of it or because you can't stand to not control your world just like my father," she said and his face flushed and she'd clearly pushed him to the edge.

"Don't you ever lump me in with your father!" Jared ground out his words. "Megan, you'd better think about an answer to this."

"I'll fight you, Jared," she declared, walking away before she turned to face him. All the old pain rushed back, memories of panicked days after he left. "I don't care how much money you have! I'm Ethan's mother. I've raised him. You walked out on us. You go ahead with your lawyers and your threats."

They glared at each other and she knew they were locked in an impasse. In spite of anguish and anger and their battle over Ethan, Jared still made her heart race. She hated herself for wanting him, when he had hurt her so badly and was trying to do it again.

"No judge will take Ethan from me," she declared, fighting her rising terror of a court battle with Jared over Ethan. "Your lifestyle will work against you, too."

"A judge has to consider my rights. I can provide Ethan with far more opportunities than you can." His words chilled her. She could never give Ethan what Jared could.

"If I walk out that door, Megan, I'm calling my attorney and I will get him started on my custody of Ethan. In the future, you'll never be able to bargain with me to the degree you can right now, so you better rethink your refusal."

"Go ahead, Jared. Bullying only makes me more certain."

"Bullying? I think I've been damn cooperative. I'm trying to find something we can both live with. You're not. You refuse to consider any arrangement."

"None are feasible. All your suggestions will hurt Ethan."

"A marriage of convenience wouldn't," Jared replied.

"I don't want to be locked into a loveless marriage with you."

Again, his face flushed and she knew his fury was increasing. "Then I know one solution. I'm calling my attorney and you'll hear from one of us, probably tomorrow morning, and the court can determine how much time each of us gets Ethan."

"Fine. I'll call my attorney now, too," she said, growing frightened and uncertain. "You're a ruthless man, Jared. I learned that too late."

"In this situation, you're forcing me to be."

"Go ahead and contact your attorney or your whole law staff. You'll have to take me to court to get your son."

"You check that out," he repeated, and strode out, not waiting. He slammed the door behind him. She stepped to the front window to watch him, his long legs covering the distance to his car quickly. He climbed into his car and sat a moment without driving away. She could see he was on his cell phone and she turned to look up the phone number of Rolf Gustavsson, her family attorney, whom she had been seeing often lately because of her father's demise.

Relieved to hear his pleasant hello, she related her problem. He said he would do some research and get back to her. Ethan's tire swing moved back and forth under a black walnut tree. It caught her eye and she ended the call.

She rubbed her temple. She knew Jared had rights. Rolf might be a nice man who had always been helpful to her family in dealing with their legal matters, but Jared had access to the world's best legal talent.

A marriage of convenience? That was impossible. Not one of his suggestions was workable. She put her head in her hands, hating that Jared had discovered Ethan.

As much as she loathed the thought of letting him have the ranch, that was better than losing Ethan to him. No way could she think of Ethan as *their* son. She had always thought of Ethan as her son only.

Now she regretted not selling the ranch to him quickly and putting as much distance as possible between them. If only—but it was too late now. The damage was done and she was going to have to live with it. She had made too many wrong decisions in her life. Was she making another one concerning Ethan?

Her head throbbed. Any joint custody she'd ever have to agree to would be ghastly to her. The fact that Jared had walked out on her had to count as a strong factor.

Halfway through the night, she decided she would offer to sell the ranch to Jared if he would forget about Ethan. It was her only hope and she hated the thought, but that would be infinitely better than having to share Ethan with him.

The rest of her sleepless night was filled with apprehension. At dawn she showered and dressed, but even sitting with a cup of coffee did nothing to shake her mood. It was too early.

When she received a call from Jared, vitality seemed to ooze from the phone.

"Good morning," he said. "I thought you'd be awake. I'd like to talk to you in person."

"Come over. I've been up for a couple of hours," she answered, hoping she sounded as upbeat as he did. She wondered what he had on his mind.

"I'll be there soon," he replied.

All too soon she heard Jared's car pull up. She went to the porch as he climbed out. Dressed in a long-sleeve, charcoal Western shirt, jeans and boots, he hurried toward the porch. Wind tangled locks of his black hair above his forehead and he looked refreshed, filled with energy, and eager—all dire implications. She smiled despite the inner turmoil that kept her stomach churning.

"Good morning," he said solemnly, studying her.

"Come inside to talk, Jared." She turned to lead the way. He closed the front door and caught up to walk with her to the family room. "Have a seat."

He nodded and they sat facing each other. The blanket of silence did nothing to soothe her raw nerves. She could tell little from his expression.

"I've heard from my attorney. Have you heard from yours?"

She shook her head. "Not yet, but mine doesn't have the resources or staff yours do, so I'm not surprised.

Jared, if you'll drop all this, I'll sell the ranch to you and you can forget the bonus one million," she said and held her breath.

He shook his head. "That wouldn't begin to take the place of getting to know my son."

Disappointment swept her and she locked her fingers together, knowing he had bad news that she didn't want to hear.

She put her hands on her face as she tried to keep from making a sound, but she couldn't prevent tears.

"Megan, don't," Jared said gently, his arms going around her. He pulled her close against him while she sobbed, letting go. "Stop crying. Plan with me and let's get an arrangement we can both live with," he said in the same gentle tone.

She knew, without waiting to hear from her lawyer, that she was going to have to do what Jared wanted.

Unable now to control her emotions after the worry of the past twenty-four hours and a sleepless night of anxiety, she sobbed and his arm around her waist tightened. He tilted her chin up and pulled out a clean handkerchief to wipe her eyes. "Stop crying," he ordered in the same quiet, gentle tone. He brushed her tears away.

He tilted her chin up to look into her eyes. "Look, you're off work anyway, and so am I. Ethan is with your relatives. Come fly with me to the Yucatán coast. I have a home there and we'll get away from interruptions for a couple of days. We're going to have to establish some kind of truce."

While she couldn't imagine spending a couple of days with him, she had to work something out or he would do as he warned. She knew Jared well enough to know that any threat he made he would carry out, if he had to.

On the other hand, they weren't going to court. He wasn't taking Ethan away. Or so he said. "I guess I don't have any other choice," she said.

"That's better. I can have a plane ready in an hour. How long will it take you to wind things up here to leave for two or three days?"

"I've never been away from Ethan, except when he's here with my relatives and I'm in Santa Fe."

"He's with them now and he'll be fine."

She nodded, becoming aware of standing in his arms. His look was heated, and under his deep focus she realized his concern was no longer about Ethan. Jared's torrid gaze made her heart drum.

She pushed against his chest and distanced herself. "All right, Jared," she said. "I can probably leave in an hour."

"I'll come pick you up. Do you have a pen? I'll give you a phone number at my house where they can reach you."

"I'll have my cell phone."

"Give me a pen. Your cell phone might fail. This way you'll have two possibilities for contact." She handed him a pen and watched him, looking at the familiar handwriting that she still could remember. When he handed a business card back to her, it had two numbers, his house and a cell phone. "Is your plane at the airport?"

"No, at the ranch," he answered.

"Then I'll drive to your place. It'll be more convenient."

He crossed the room to her, to slip his arms around her waist. "Stop worrying, Megan. We'll work something out and I'll do my damnedest to win his love and to get to know him. I want what's best for Ethan, too."

If he really wanted what was best for Ethan, he would stay out of Ethan's life. But she knew she had to stop fighting Jared, because it was hopeless. The law was on his side. "I'll work on it," she whispered.

"No, you stop worrying," he ordered, but his voice was gentle and quiet. "I promise, I'll try if you will to find a viable solution."

Unable to speak, afraid she would start crying again, she nodded. "I had better get ready."

"Okay, but I wish you could smile." He knelt slightly to be on eye level, smiling at her, and teased a half-hearted smile from her. "That's better. I'm going to try to get a real smile out of you while we're together."

She didn't want to go away with him. She wanted to tell him that she still thought he was ruthless and arrogant and had to have his way, but it was useless. She followed him outside, and the minute they parted she rushed back into the house to call Rolf.

"Rolf, thanks so much. I'll deal with Jared. He is willing to work something out."

She finally got off the phone to put her head into her hands and cry. She didn't want any of this.

In minutes, she called her aunt to tell her what had happened and that she was going with Jared for a few days. She choked back the tears when she talked to

Ethan, but he never noticed. He'd gotten a new electronic game and when she told him she was going away, he accepted it with barely a pause in his chatter about the game.

Knowing he was in good hands, she said good-bye and hurried to change and pack.

She dressed in brown slacks, a matching sleeveless top and wore high-heeled sandals. Brushing her hair, she clipped it high on the back of her head.

She was going away with Jared to one of his secluded homes. She could well imagine what he had in mind. Along with arranging custody plans was a plan for seduction.

She didn't want to return after several days with him, not only losing rights to her son, but in love with Jared—twice in her life.

And Jared might be the sexiest, most charming man she'd ever known.

She would have to keep up her guard. So far, she had failed miserably in all dealings with him.

By a quarter past eleven, she was airborne, flying over Jared's ranch and headed south. To avoid conversation with him, she gazed out the window, looking at his ranch spread below. She turned back to find him watching her. Dressed in chinos, a charcoal knit shirt and loafers, he looked commanding, as if satisfied with all facets of his world. And why wouldn't he, she thought. He'd won the first part of their fight.

"This is a hopeful start, Megan," he said, leaning close to touch a wispy lock of hair that had come free from her tie.

"You're an incredible optimist," she said.

"If we work something out, then there's no problem."

"I know you already have something in mind," she said stiffly.

He shrugged. "Not necessarily. Let's let it go for today and get back on better footing with each other," he suggested.

"If we can," she said, looking out the window while fighting the urge to scream that she hadn't planned on a better relationship with him, but she knew she had to now. Getting concessions from him on the custody front could be impossible otherwise.

"Of course, we can," he said, taking her hand. "I've got three days with a beautiful woman, who I intend to get to know."

"You know me well enough," she said, gazing into his dark eyes that hid his intentions and thoughts.

"No, I don't. I knew an eighteen-year-old. You've changed. You're far more poised, more self-assured and much more unattainable."

"I suppose that comes with growing up, although, when I met you, you had all the confidence imaginable."

He gave her a crooked smile. "Does that mean arrogance? That's what it sounds like."

She had to smile in return. "Definitely. But I'd like to stay on your good side as much as possible on this trip, so I'm trying to be polite."

"Don't be polite with me. But staying on my good side—that's fine. What are your plans for the future,

Megan? Do you intend to always keep your gallery in
Santa Fe, even if you divide your days between there
and the ranch?"

"Yes. Santa Fe is home and perfect for us," she said,
aware her hand was still in his, as he ran his thumb back
and forth over her wrist. His touches added fuel to the
lust she battled.

"I love Santa Fe," she continued, "and I never want
to move from there. I always hoped Ethan would grow
up and stay nearby, but that isn't realistic, I know. Now
that he'll have time with you, heaven knows what he'll
do when he's grown."

"That's far away," Jared said. "Do you like to
swim?"

"Actually, I love to. I guess because there was
little chance to when I was growing up, and then
there aren't many opportunities in Santa Fe. I don't
have a suit, though. There's no need to keep one at
the ranch."

"We'll stop and I'll get you one."

"I'll buy my suit," she said, laughing.

He smiled. "That's better," he said, touching the
corner of her mouth and running his finger lightly along
her lower lip, building a warmth in her. "I promise to
get a real laugh out of you before the night is over."

"Stick to why we're here, Jared," she said quietly.
"This is an interlude to work out a plan for our future
concerning Ethan. It's not to get reacquainted all over
again. Not at all."

"What's wrong with renewing a friendship?" he asked.

"It was more than a friendship, and I don't want a

broken heart twice," she said, hoping she never hurt again as badly as she had the year he left.

"I promise, I don't intend to hurt you," he said.

"Then keep these few days relatively impersonal. I'm working at this, Jared. Don't make it complicated and more difficult," she instructed briskly.

"I wouldn't think of it," he said, once again leaning back in his chair. "So, tell me about a typical day in your life. What do you and Ethan do?"

"Through the school year, Ethan is in a private school and I spend most of the day in my studio. I have someone who runs the gallery for me, except on Wednesdays and Fridays, when I run it myself. I have three salespeople who work in the gallery for me at different hours, not all at the same time, but there are always two of us present. It's easier that way."

"I haven't been to Santa Fe in years. Not since you moved there. What's the name of your gallery?" he asked, locking his fingers behind his head and stretching out his long legs. Looking totally relaxed, he reminded her of a leopard or tiger, some large cat lazing and half asleep, yet able to pounce in a flash. Except Jared would never physically pounce. His methods were emotional and mental. "Wait, let me guess," he said. "Sorenson Gallery."

"Am I that unimaginative?" she asked, smiling at him. He smiled in return. "I toyed with some less ordinary names, but when I opened it, it was all new and exciting, and I was trying to get established and make a name for myself, so it became Sorenson Gallery. That was about the same year you opened your first restaurant in Dallas—Dalton's, I believe."

"I used my name for the same reason you did," he said quietly. "You kept up, did you?"

She shrugged. "My aunt and uncle knew people who knew your family, so word got around. In some ways we're in a small world."

"One that got far more interesting when you came back into my life," he added.

"Jared, is it possible for you to avoid flirting?"

"Not with you," he replied with an enticing smile. He leaned forward. "You look elegant, but there's one flaw."

"Oh, what's that?" she asked, trying not to care, yet aware how close he was again.

"You would look much better," he said and reached up to remove the clip holding her hair, "without this." Her thick curtain of black hair tumbled on her shoulders and back. "There, that's perfect," he said.

She smiled and shook her head to get her hair away from her face. "You may like it better, but it's not as convenient."

"I definitely like it better. Sacrifice convenience to please mc. I'll appreciate it."

"How's the weather where we're headed?"

"It's beautiful. Perfect, too."

"Enough of that!" she retorted, his compliment pleasing her.

She settled back and listened, chatting with him, laughing at some of his stories. The day passed surprisingly fast, and she realized she was enjoying his company, even though each minute with him brought back memories of being together. Too often, she dreaded when they got to the point of this trip.

"We must be getting close." The deep blue of the Gulf caught her eye. "Are you in town?"

"No. I have a villa on the coast. We'll have total privacy."

"I don't think we'll require total privacy, but it'll be nice."

It was a long trip, but eventually they landed and deplaned, and Jared escorted her to a limo where his chauffeur and bodyguard stood waiting.

Within minutes, Jared and Megan were driven into town to a small, exclusive shop to look for a swimsuit. While Jared stood near the front window and talked on his cell phone, she was shown a variety of suits. Selecting a half dozen, she tried them on without showing them to Jared. She made her selection and dressed again, emerging from the dressing room.

"I didn't get to see you model the suits," Jared said with a twinkle in his eyes.

"You'll see me soon enough when you swim with me."

"I'm counting the minutes," he said, and she smiled.

"Always flirting, Jared. If we aren't fighting," she amended.

"I hope to be done with the latter," he said, and there was a solemn note in his voice that made her feel he was sincere in wanting to work something out in cooperation. She remembered he was a master at convincing people to do what he wanted, and wondered if his words were shallow or really held meaning.

For a moment she gazed into his brown eyes and had a pang of longing for what could have been between them. Shaking off the wishful thinking, she started to open her purse.

Stopping her, Jared took the suit from her hand. "I'll get this," he said in a tone that ended her argument.

As she watched, Jared purchased two more identical ones.

She laughed. "Jared, I'm not in a swim contest. I only need one suit."

"You never know. Always be prepared. Why not?"

"Because it's a waste of your money," she said, wondering about his extravagant lifestyle, and how much Ethan's life was about to change. And perhaps her own.

"Then let me worry about it," he said, smiling at her. She stopped protesting.

They drove out of town and thick trees and bushes crowded the narrow highway until they turned into iron gates and Jared waved at a man who returned the greeting.

"How often are you here?" Megan asked.

"A few weeks out of the year. He's a gatekeeper, and I let him know we were coming. The staff is here now."

Curious about Jared's life, she wondered if he was showing her this home to prove that he could do more for Ethan than she could. Yet it didn't feel like a jab. His pride in his home shone through. They drove through more thick vegetation and then through another set of gates that swung open at the limo's approach. A high plaster wall glowed pale yellow, with patterns of shade from tall trees close by. Past the gates, the surroundings transformed into a garden paradise. Palms, other tropical trees and plants dotted the emerald grass.

Beautifully landscaped lawns led to a sprawling white villa with the brilliant blue water of the ocean as a backdrop. Blue trumpet-shaped blossoms of tall jacaranda trees were bright in the sunlight.

"Jared, it's fantastic!" she said, awed. She was certain now that he wanted to impress her with how much more he could do for Ethan than she.

"I enjoy it. I hope you do, too. How about a swim first thing?"

"That sounds wonderful." She conceded. "A swim after the long flight is exactly what I need." In the flash of pleasure she released her hold on their problems momentarily.

"Swim it is," he said. "Unpack later, or I can have Lupita do it for you."

"I'll unpack myself, thank you," she replied in amusement. "I really can't wait."

"I can't wait, either," he said in a husky voice that registered with her, and she glanced at him.

"You don't swim often?" she said, as if deliberately missing his meaning.

"I want to see you in your suit."

"Oh, stop!" She turned back to look at the house and its porch, with pots of lavender orchids. Yellow and scarlet bougainvillea ran up the walls and onto the roof. "Jared, this is magical." Feeling a pang when she thought about Jared bringing Ethan to see it.

"I'm glad you think so."

As soon as they parked, a uniformed man emerged from the house. Jared introduced her to Adan, who took their bags. Inside, she met Lupita, who smiled broadly and listened to brief instructions from Jared.

As Megan walked through the front door, her breath caught. The entry was wide and open with columns. Extended beyond the entrance was a large living area she could see through open, floor-to-ceiling glass doors and bamboo furniture.

Beyond the room, through the open doors, was a veranda that extended to a sparkling, aqua pool with a fountain and waterfall. The deck over continued to a glistening white beach and on to the ocean.

"Jared, this is incredible."

"I told you, I think so, too," he said, walking up to her. "Get your suit and I'll meet you outside."

She looked up to meet his gaze, and the air between them crackled from the attraction. Her nerves were raw, her desire hot. Drawing a deep breath, she stepped away. "Where's my room?"

He escorted her along a hallway and his fingers rested lightly on her arm.

He led her into another room that opened onto the veranda and had a view of the ocean. He paused. "How's this?"

She looked at the rattan furniture, with its yellow-and-white-chintz cushions, and at a ceiling fan turning lazily overhead. "This is beautiful, Jared. It looks like a house staged for a movie."

"Nope, it's ready for living. I'll meet you at the pool." He traced his knuckles along her cheek. "This is good, Meg. We don't have to be at odds with each other. I know we can find common ground and be friends."

"That's what *you* want," she reminded him, her pulse racing from his touch. With a twist of longing, she wished she could drop her guard, trust him again and be friends.

He flashed her a smile and left, stepping outside through the open doors.

She looked at a king-size bed with a white spread, and then she explored a spacious bathroom with a sunken tub, potted palms and a wall of mirrors. She returned to the bedroom to open her sacks of purchases she'd made in town.

After she changed, she studied herself in the mirror with a critical eye. She'd known she would swim with Jared and she didn't want anything skimpy. Without encouragement of any kind from her, he came on strong. He'd spent the day flirting, yet no matter how casual his touches, each contact sizzled.

She had bought a navy one-piece that covered her as much as possible and still looked nice, because she wouldn't be wearing it with Jared after this week. Also, she'd bought a navy cover-up and flip-flops. When she was dressed, she went out through the open doors, stepping onto the veranda and heading toward the pool.

Watching Jared swim to one end of the pool, she kicked off her flip-flops and shed her cover-up. He paused to shake water off his face and rake his hair back with his fingers. As always when damp, his hair curled and short locks sprang back, curling on his forehead. As soon as he saw her, he swam across the pool, causing a

big splash of water when he lifted himself out on the side
of the pool.

Water glistened on his shoulders and chest and body.
The thick mat of black curls on his chest was covered
with drops of water. At the sight of his lean, muscled
body, even more fit than when she'd known him in his
twenties, her temperature climbed. His swimsuit was a
narrow strip of black that covered little. Too well she
remembered exactly how he had looked aroused and
nude. She realized how she was looking at him and
glanced up to see his gaze roaming slowly over her. And
she knew she'd made another colossal miscalculation
by traveling here with him.

Six

As he walked to her, her heart pounded.

"Jared," she whispered. There was some dim protest echoing in her thoughts, but she paid no heed.

He walked up to take her into his arms and draw her to him. The scanty clothing they wore was nothing. She was pressed against his muscled body, his warm, wet chest, his strong thighs. Every inch she touched was hard and firm. When his gaze lowered to her mouth, her lips parted.

"Jared," she repeated softly.

He leaned down and she raised her mouth to his, his lips covering hers and then his tongue slipped into her mouth as he kissed her. Her insides clenched while insistent need swept her, pooling low. She wound her arms around his neck and clung to him, kissing him hungrily, beyond caring about the danger to her feelings. He was temptation and excitement and sizzling sex.

As they kissed, she ran her fingers through his thick hair and along the strong column of his neck, savoring, exploring every inch of him.

His arm tightened around her, pressing her intimately to his firmness and her heart pounded.

Holding her, he caressed her nape before sliding his hand down to push away her suit and cup her breast. He rubbed his palm lightly in circles over her nipple.

Moaning with pleasure, she arched against him, tingling and wanting more. Running her hand along his smooth, bare back, she pressed her hips against him.

"Ah, Meg, so fine," he whispered. Lowering the top of her suit fully, he held both breasts in his hands. His thumbs circled each taut peak and his hot gaze was as scalding as his touch. While she slid one hand to his waist, her other hand gripped his broad shoulder.

Desire was explosive. She knew what they could do to each other, and she wanted to rediscover him. When her hand skimmed along his thigh, drifting up over his hip and down his flat belly, she heard his intake of breath.

Stirring a shower of tingles, his hand played lightly on her stomach and between her legs, his fingers inching beneath the suit to touch her intimately.

"Jared! Yes!" she cried, thrusting against his touch, clinging to his upper arms as his fingers created a tantalizing friction.

She was lost, spiraling into a vortex of hunger and memory. She couldn't stop. All her being cried out for him. Searing need burned like wildfire. He traced circles around her nipple with his tongue, as dazzling sensations showered her.

"Jared!" she cried, unaware she'd spoken.

Gasping for breath, she pushed away his suit, freeing him. Bending to take him into her mouth, her tongue circled the velvet tip of his manhood.

His fingers wound in her hair and he groaned. She hoped to make him as desperate for her as she was for him.

Stroking him with her tongue, she caressed his inner thighs, running her hands between his legs. He groaned again and then his hands went beneath her arms and he lifted her to her feet and plunged his gaze into hers, his broad chest expanding with his breath.

He scooped her into his arms and carried her to a chaise lounge to place her on it and sit beside her, tracing feathery kisses along her collarbone to her breasts, sucking and biting each nipple lightly, an exquisite torment for her.

"Oh! I want you. Heaven help me, how I want you!" she blurted.

His hand was between her legs, caressing her, rubbing her and starting to build tension all over again. Then he moved between her legs to place them over his shoulders and give himself access to her, his tongue retracing his fingers' path.

She squeezed her eyes closed tightly, as she was bombarded by sensations. She was open for him, eager, intensity building with each stroke of his tongue.

"Love me," she cried as he lowered her legs to the chaise.

"I'll get protection," he said, picking her up. He carried her with him through open doors and laid her gently on the bed.

She watched as he retrieved a condom from the bedside table. Caressing her inner thighs, he moved between her legs. Wanting him with increasing urgency, she stroked his strong legs.

While he opened the packet and put on the condom, she drank in the sight of him, storing the moment in memory, relishing looking at him and touching him. Virile, muscled, and bronze except for a pale strip across his groin, he was masculine perfection. Thick black curls spread on his chest, tapering in a narrow line to his waist. Short crisp hair curled on his thighs. Locks of black hair fell over his forehead. His body was marvelous.

As she looked up into his dark eyes, magnetism sparked between them from a mutual feeling of attraction and something deeper, a tenuous bond held for the moment, created by sheer physical longing.

In a silent welcoming, she held out her arms. While he kissed her, she wrapped her arms around him.

Jared was in her arms again, consuming her. Time didn't exist. How she had hungered for this moment!

Driven, she pulled him toward her. When he entered her, she arched her hips to meet him. Making love with him enveloped her and smoothed over problems. She wrapped her long legs around him and ran her hands over his smooth back, and then his firm buttocks.

For this brief moment, their union seemed right, incredibly necessary for her. She held him tightly, running her hands over him again, relishing the feel of his body and that he was in her arms.

Moving her hips against him, she groaned with pleasure. He filled her slowly, withdrawing and then entering her again, in a sweet torment that heightened her need to a raging inferno.

His powerful body was spectacular. She clung to him, mindlessly raking his back with her fingers, moving faster beneath him.

"Jared!" she cried his name, unaware of anything except his loving. She moved frantically.

His control vanished and he moved rapidly, pumping deeply into her. They were locked together—rocking, intimate and close, and she sobbed because she wanted him with all her being.

"Meg, darlin'." He ground out the words in a husky voice. His endearment made her heart leap, and she knew she was vulnerable in too many ways. His words were as seductive to her as his lovemaking. Physically and emotionally, she wanted him.

She climaxed in a shattering release. Lights exploded behind her closed eyelids while her heart pounded violently. Ecstasy enveloped her as spasms rocked her. He pumped faster, and then groaned, reaching his own finish, still pleasuring her.

He inhaled deeply and slowed and she could feel tension winding up once again. She tightened her arms and legs around him again.

"Jared," she cried softly, "don't stop loving me," she whispered as he thrust slower, and as it commenced another building, sweet torment. Impaled on his thick rod, she moved her hips faster. And then another climax rocked her with rapture.

She hugged him, feeling the sheen of sweat on his back. They held each other tightly, returning to earth from a distant paradise.

Reality was a wolf at the door, and she didn't want to face tomorrow's problems.

He turned on his side, untangling his long legs from hers. She pressed tightly against him, her face against his throat with her head on his shoulder. Deliberately, she kept her mind blank, relishing the euphoria and lethargy after lovemaking.

He shifted, then tilted up her chin so he could look into her eyes. "Loving you is fantastic, Meg."

"Shh." She put her finger over his lips. "Don't talk. Don't do anything for a few minutes," she urged. She agreed privately, but she wasn't going to confess what she'd experienced.

He was quiet, gazing at her solemnly while she traced his jaw with her fingers, letting her hand caress his chest lightly. He sucked in a deep breath and gently combed her hair away from her face while he showered light kisses on her.

"You're fabulous," he said in a husky voice, shifting away again to brush his fingers across her bare breasts.

She caught his hand in hers, trailing kisses over his knuckles, still refusing to think about anything except the present moment.

Rolling onto his back, he drew her close in his embrace, remaining quiet, as she had asked. She tangled her fingers in his chest hair and then let her hand

slide over him to his waist. His body was in peak con-
dition, a marvel to her.

As she shifted, starting to sit up, his strong arms
held her. "Where are you going?" he asked.

"To shower," she said.

He sat up. "I'll shower, too," he said and she shook
her head.

"Jared, we've—"

His arm circled her waist and his mouth covered
hers, taking her words. He kissed her deeply, lowering
her to the bed. Once again, she knew now was the
moment to stop him, but she was already responding
to him as if they hadn't just made love.

When he raised his head, she opened her eyes to find
him watching her. Standing to pick her up, he was hard
again, ready for love. While he gazed into her eyes, he
carried her into the shower and turned on warm water.

As he lowered her feet to the floor, he leaned forward
to kiss her. Desiring him more than ever, she wrapped her
arms around his neck, leaning into him. Their bodies were
wet, warm, pressed against each other while her heart
raced. Desire rekindled, quickly reaching a raging fire.

Jared's arousal was hot against her belly. She
moaned softly. It had been so long since she had been
loved by him, and he was the only one, something she
never intended for him to know. Worse, she couldn't get
enough, now that she had let go.

He picked her up, stepped back to brace himself
against the glass wall of the shower and then lowered
her onto himself.

She cried out with pleasure, throwing her head back,

running one hand over his shoulder as she moved with him and he thrust fast, taking her quickly.

She squeezed her eyes closed, gasping for breath, holding his shoulders tightly now while he kissed her.

"Love, this is good," he whispered, but she heard him as she had before.

"Love me," she whispered, wanting him.

In ecstasy once more, she climaxed as he climaxed. She draped herself on his shoulders, kissing his neck and caressing him, running her hands lightly on his shoulders and back.

He would break her heart again. She knew that clearly. She couldn't refuse to face the truth. Fighting all the tender feelings toward him that surged in her, she turned away.

"Meg, darlin', this is fine. So fine," he said in his deep voice. "You're magic, pure seduction, beautiful."

His words were golden, taking her heart as he had once before. She raised her head to meet his gaze. "Put me down, Jared."

He set her on her feet and pulled her against him to kiss her until she responded fully. "You don't know what you do to me," he said.

She would lose any battle with him, she realized. Why had she ever thought she could successfully contend with him and win? She was consumed by his lovemaking—boneless and unable to think straight.

He showered light kisses on her shoulder, drawing his tongue over the curves of her ear. Still kissing her and holding his arm around her waist while he caressed her, he walked her backward beneath the spray of water. He smiled. "This is perfect."

His smile softened his features, lending a warmth to his expression that had been missing too much since he'd come back into her life.

She smiled in return, a part of her responding, a part of her knowing she was flying into disaster at the speed of light.

"You're a charming devil," she said, shaking her head.

"And you're a seductress. Pure temptation." He took one step back and his hands rested on her waist while his gaze slowly traveled over her.

She couldn't keep from studying him as thoroughly and intently as he was her. His body was magnificent, radiating vitality and energy.

"I know something better," he said, switching off the water. He opened the door to grab thick, soft terry-cloth towels off a shelf. He handed her a blue towel and began to dry her with his towel. In turn, she dried him, running the towel over his broad shoulders, his muscled chest.

His strokes were light, a slow, sensual friction rubbing her nipples. Then he dried her belly and the insides of her thighs, then he ran the towel between her legs lightly.

She gasped, pausing in her task, grasping his arms. "Jared!" she whispered.

"I'm only drying you," he said, continuing. "Come here." He picked her up and carried her easily out of the shower and set her on her feet in front of the mirrored wall. He gazed over her head. "We look right together. You're more beautiful than ever," he whispered, standing close behind her and letting his hands play over her stomach and breasts. As he watched her in the mirror, he cupped her breasts and began to tease her nipples. Longing flared, and she wanted him again.

She started to kiss him, but he held her. "Wait," he whispered. "Look at us. Look what I can do to you," he added, cupping her breasts as he ran his thumbs in circles over her nipples.

"You can do too much to me," she whispered. His hands were tan against her pale skin. His caresses were torment and she wanted him inside her again. She spread her legs, her heart pounding, while she tugged at his arm and hand, but he wouldn't stop what he was doing.

He continued to caress her breast with one hand while his other drifted between her legs to touch her intimately. While she moved her hips, she reached behind her to touch him in any manner she could, knowing she was violating all her promises to herself.

"Jared, you have to..." she began, but he leaned closer, kissing her shoulder and ear, and her words ceased.

His hand between her thighs was torment. She spread her legs wider, giving him access to her as she moved her hips and as tension wound as tight as a spring.

"Wait!" she said, clutching his arms. "We can't do this!"

"We're doing it," he whispered into her ear. "You're setting me on fire, Meg," he added in another harsh whisper.

She wanted him inside her now more than ever.

He kissed her, then picked her up and carried her to bed to love her slowly, tantalizing her until her climax was more dazzling than before.

Afterward, as they were locked in each other's embrace, she was quiet until she started to ease away.

He held her tightly with one arm. "Where are you going?"

"To my room, Jared."

"Stay here awhile," he said. "I want to hold you close. I need you here, Meg," he said.

She did as he asked and lay quietly while he turned on his side to look at her and brush her hair away from her face. "I want to look at you," he whispered.

Unable to answer him, she ran her hand lightly across his chest. Regrets grew, threatening to overwhelm her. Finally she sat up and pulled a sheet up over her. "Jared, I've been too vulnerable."

He lay on his back to study her. "Don't regret what happened. It was fantastic, and no harm to either of us."

She shook her head, looking away so she wouldn't have to gaze into his dark brown eyes that seemed to see right into her thoughts. "Don't say anything, Jared. It's over. I haven't been with a man in a long, long time. You're incredibly seductive and I have a weakness where you're concerned, which you know. Once we started, I wanted it as much as you did. I'm not blaming you for our lovemaking, but it's done. Really ended. We're going to have to work something out about Ethan, but we're not going to become bed partners or marry for the convenience of it."

"Why not? We're good in bed, and you said it yourself—we enjoy each other. An understatement when it comes to the sex. It's the best."

She was struggling to get distance back between

them, knowing too well how easily he could overcome her opposition. But she intended to declare her feelings and let him know what she wanted the most. And it wasn't his lovemaking.

"I told you, I succumbed today, when I really didn't intend for that to happen between us. It complicates life."

"It simplifies it immeasurably, and it adds a spectacular dimension to living."

She turned to look into his eyes. "Don't you get it? You broke my heart—and I won't go through that again. We made love today because I've never *had* another man in my life, only you!" She flung the words at him angrily and saw his eyes widen in surprise.

"There was never anyone who could measure up. Even when I planned to sleep with someone—I couldn't go through with it. You know Mike and I never consummated our marriage, but there wasn't anyone else, either. That's why I was so damned vulnerable to your kisses today. It won't happen again, so don't plan on it. We're here to work out something about Ethan. Nothing else, in spite of what's happened today."

Breathing erratically, she stood and yanked the sheet off the bed, wrapping it around her.

He got off the bed, but she shook her head and backed away. "Don't touch me," she said, and he stopped, frowning as he watched her.

"Megan, when I left, I hurt and I hated it."

"Oh, you hurt, too?" she said, shaking her head. "Cry me a river. Let's not dredge up even more anguish. I'll shower and then I'm going for a swim."

As she hurried out of the room, tears stung her eyes and she didn't know whether she was crying out of frustration or anger.

Hopefully, now she no longer would, and she could deal with him on a more rational basis. She knew, in spite of her admonitions, he would continue to caress and flirt, because that was as natural to him as breathing. If only she could get this trip over with and something tolerable worked out!

As she went outside to retrieve her cover-up and her suit, she wondered where his staff was, but at the moment she barely cared. She'd never see them again after these few days.

She hurried to shower and in minutes jumped into the pool to swim laps, hoping to work off her emotional turmoil and restore her normal perspective.

Seven

"Let me help you out. We can swim in the ocean. It's warm and buoyant, and if you see fish, they're tropical and beautiful." Lost in the rhythm of her laps, she'd missed Jared's approach.

She gave him her hand and he pulled her up easily onto the side of the pool. He placed his hands on her waist. "Let me really look at this suit. It's great, but it covers a lot."

"Jared, we're getting far away from working out our problems. They're still present."

"Lighten up, Megan," he said easily. "It won't hurt to drop them for tonight and get back on friendlier footing."

"I can's shut off my worries the way you can," she replied swiftly, thinking about Ethan and the prospect of having him cut out of a big chunk of her life. "Kisses and moonlight swims don't gain us anything."

"Yes, they do," he argued solemnly, stepping closer. "If we can get some kind of friendship and cooperation, it'll help. We're in this together, to some degree, for a long time to come. Tonight, let go of your worries. Ethan's safe and happy. You won't help him by staying aloof and worrying. C'mon. Try to be friends."

"That's a strange thing to say after making love to me," she said, yet she realized he had a point, and her worrying tonight wasn't going to solve her problems. "It's just hard to let go when I'm filled with concern."

He caressed her cheek. "I'm sure it is," he said gently, making her want to plead her case again, but she knew that was pointless.

"You win for now. I'll try, but I can't let go of my anxiety."

"I'll try to help. Come on. A good swim will remove a little stress," he said, leading her toward the beach.

"There's someone's yacht anchored not far out," she noticed, looking at the sun splashing over a dazzling white boat.

"It's mine, and right now no one's on it. It's wired with alarms, so it doesn't have to have someone there constantly. That's two things money can buy—security and privacy."

"Race you to the floating dock," he said, while he tossed their towels onto the warm sand.

She ran with him and knew he was keeping pace with her, because he could easily outrun her. He released her hand when they were in knee-deep water and she continued to splash on, surprised how far the shallow water extended. When it deepened, Jared jumped in to swim.

She followed, knowing he would easily reach the dock first. When he did, he gave her a hand and pulled her up beside him and she raked her wet hair back from her face.

"The water is perfect and so beautiful."

"What's beautiful is you," he said, turning to place his hand behind her head.

"Jared—"

"Shh, Meg. One kiss isn't catastrophic," he said, his gaze lowering to her mouth. Her pulse drummed as he leaned down to cover her mouth with his.

"Not to you," she whispered, before his lips covered hers. Then he kissed her and she wound her arm around his neck and kissed him in return. Finally she pushed away.

"Stop—and remember what I told you."

With a hungry look that was filled with desire, he released her and sat beside her. She wrinkled her nose at him.

"Besides, I don't want you to interfere with my swim."

She expected one of his light remarks. Instead, he gave her a somber look, and she couldn't imagine what he was thinking.

"Jared, today has been unique, a temporary truce and lull, and I love your home and I love swimming. But all this is simply postponing the inevitable."

"I know, but I thought it would be best if we got on better footing with each other."

"We've done that, all right," she quipped.

"It's better than arguing," he said quietly. "Also, it gives each of us more of a chance to think things through."

She knew she would remember this day the rest of her life. She'd remember Jared sitting beside her, drops of water glistening on his bronze shoulders and body, the warm sun shining and cool water lapping around them, the beach and house in sight—a dream that was real.

"After dinner, we'll give it another go."

She nodded, knowing this was an illusion of peace and compatibility. In spite of the past few hours, their relationship was stormier than ever.

"Well, I came planning to swim, so I'll swim," she said, turning to look at the yellow buoys bobbing several hundred yards farther out. "It's safe to the buoys?" she asked.

"That's right."

She jumped in and swam, and in seconds he swam beside her, eventually swimming back to shore. She walked out and spread a towel to sit cross-legged in the sand, and he did the same.

"That was fantastic. The water is perfect. I may have to think about some kind of place like this for myself. It would be good for Ethan because he's not much of a swimmer, but he likes the water."

Jared stood and extended his hand. "If you're ready to go in, we'll dress and I'll tell Lupita to put on dinner."

"Where is Lupita? I haven't seen anyone since we first arrived."

"The staff knows how to stay out of sight. She'll get dinner on and then go for the night. They have homes in this compound, but beyond the security walls. There's nothing inside the walls except my house, its outbuildings and us."

At the veranda, he paused. "I'll go find Lupita and meet you here in half an hour and we can have a drink before dinner."

She nodded and headed for her room.

Finally clad in a black knit shirt and black slacks, Jared looked dark, handsome and dangerous. He was a threat to her future and he wasn't going to go away and let her live her life the way she had before.

Jared crossed the veranda to take her hands while his gaze drifted lazily over her. "You look beautiful. Far more tempting than dinner."

She waved her hand dismissively. "Thank you, Jared."

"What would you like to drink?"

"A piña colada, please, if that's possible."

"Quite possible," Jared replied, moving around behind a bar to get bottles of light and dark rum that he poured into a blender, adding other ingredients and mixing them with crushed ice. He poured the drink into a hurricane glass and handed it to her, getting a cold beer for himself. Taking her chilled glass, she moved to a chair to sit and gaze at the ocean. The sun was a huge fiery ball, low on the horizon.

"Will you bring Ethan here?" she asked.

"I'll take him everywhere," Jared said. She felt the hurt again.

"I always thought about taking him places, but I thought I should wait until he's older. I suppose I waited too long."

"Nonsense. You can still go where you want with

him," Jared said. "You can come with us, if you want to," he said.

She turned to him. "Jared, today was lust. It was sexual, meaningless, nothing more. It didn't bind us together in any manner except physically. My feelings toward you haven't changed. And your feelings are no kinder toward me than mine are toward you."

He set his drink on a table. "That's not so. I think there was more to this afternoon than you'll admit or recognize because you're still angry with me. We can both come here and bring Ethan with us and have a wonderful escape," he said.

She shook her head. "No. That won't work, Jared. Not really. Today was no indicator of the future."

He looked annoyed, and then he seemed to visibly relax. "You're cutting yourself out of some good moments," Jared said.

"I'll manage."

"Dinner is served," Lupita announced, her voice cutting through the tense moment.

"Thanks, Lupita," Jared said, standing to take Megan's arm to stroll to another section of the veranda where it curved around a wing of the house. Tall palms lined their patio, and potted palms and banana trees gave the appearance of being in a garden by the sea.

With candles burning despite the daylight, the glass-and-iron table set with colorful china and sparkling crystal was ready for a photo shoot. On the table was an appetizer of escargot, while steaming, covered dishes waited next to it. Jared held her chair, his hand drifting lightly to her nape and then he sat himself across from her, smiling at her.

"I don't know how you ever leave this and go back to Texas."

"It's too quiet except for a few days at a time. I'm too active and like to work. I imagine you'd feel the same if you were here for weeks. The first visit, I stayed a month. I haven't lasted that long since."

She could well imagine that he always brought a woman with him. Just as he had with her. Trying to avoid the subject burning inside her, she chatted with him over dinner of jambalaya, fluffy golden asiago biscuits and melons, mango and kiwi with Gorgonzola cheese. Dessert was thin slices of cheesecake flown in from Miami. Pale slices were drizzled with chocolate and raspberry sauce. Dinner was delectable, their conversation innocuous, but his gaze clearly conveyed smoldering desire.

"Dinner is delicious. Are you trying to soften me up in all possible ways?"

"You're soft and warm now, each luscious inch," he said, smiling at her.

"I walked into that one. Thank you, Jared. Those compliments come so easily to you, you must not even think about what you're saying."

"Not so, Meg," he said, caressing her hand. "Being together is good. I see great hope for the future."

As the sun vanished and darkness enveloped them, lanterns and outdoor lighting automatically came on over the veranda and along the beach. The flickering light highlighted the planes of Jared's face, his straight nose and prominent cheekbones.

"Let's move where it's comfortable," he suggested, and she nodded.

While she chatted with Jared, Lupita and Adan cleared and said good night.

"It's difficult to imagine that you require a body-guard."

"I think I should hire one for you, and I know Ethan is going to have to have one." Jared leaned forward. "His life is going to change and you can't stop it. There are things that go along with my wealth. Paparazzi, the possibility of kidnapping."

She flinched and looked away, hating everything that was happening to her life and to Ethan's. "If only I had sold the ranch to you. You would never have known about Ethan," she said bitterly.

"It's too late for that now."

"Jared, try to understand. I've told you before and I'll say it again—you have an extravagant lifestyle that doesn't make you good daddy material."

"I won't be that way with Ethan. Give me some credit here," he replied with a stubborn just of his chin.

"You do wild things like mountain climbing. I know you used to do bronc riding in rodeos," she said, elic-iting a brief smile from him.

"I haven't ridden in years. I gave that up when I graduated from college. And I won't take him moun-tain climbing."

"I don't want him jet-setting all over the world with you."

"I'll be reasonable about travel, too, but there are places I'll want to take him, like where I'm taking you now."

"Some places I can get used to," she said, locking her fingers together. "Jared, I've been so close with Ethan. I guess I hover, and I may be overprotective, but I love him with all my heart. Except for my pottery, he's my whole world. And he comes first. It just hurts to think I have to share him. As much as I hate to admit it, I feel I'm losing him."

Jared nodded. "I understand, Megan. That's why I've suggested things like the marriage of convenience. And remember, you willingly shared him with your aunt and uncle."

"That's part of the problem. I share him with them, and now I'll have to divide my time with you. I'll lose being with him a lot."

"Yes, you will, but let's try to find the most workable way—and I'm not averse to having you around when I'm with him."

"It's just incredibly difficult to give up my child," she said.

"You won't have to give him up if you'll work with me. There are some things that come with the territory, though, and I know you want to keep him safe. How you've managed to hide his paternity from the world all these years, I'll never know. Whose name is on the birth certificate? It can't be that ex-husband of yours, because he never adopted Ethan."

"It is Mike's name. My dad paid to get that taken care of by some doctor in Chicago. It may be illegal, but I have a birth certificate claiming Mike as Ethan's father."

"Well, we'll get that straightened out, but the minute

word gets out about his tie to me—and you become part of my life again, even if we're not on the best of terms— you both will be vulnerable. You might as well have a chauffeur—"

She laughed in this first truly humorous moment since Jared came back into her life. "A chauffeur! In Santa Fe!"

He grinned. "I finally got a laugh out of you, and that's great, Meg. It's good to hear you laugh again."

"I'll become the town oddity."

"No, you won't. There are more people chauffeured around Santa Fe than you think. Famous and wealthy people live there. You don't pay attention to things like that."

"He'll want to tell his best friend."

"Tell away. His friends will meet the guy. Give a thought to schools, too. I can afford whatever you want."

"I'm not sending my six-year-old away to school. He's in private school now, and I do schoolwork with him."

"I can afford tutors, too, if you want them. Same with lessons. I'll pay for all that. As for the bodyguard, you'll be on the ranch part of the year, so you're incredibly vulnerable there because of the isolation. I'll get someone who'll be discreet. You should also have a guard on the premises."

"You're being generous," she said. Every suggestion tore at her. Even if it was best for Ethan, it would change his life.

"Now, what can we work out about his visitation?" Jared asked.

She glanced at him. "What about if you get him Saturdays and Sundays and we alternate holidays," she
finally suggested, hating the thought of losing Ethan on
weekends. "Though I don't know how he can play on
the soccer team or basketball or baseball or anything
else if he goes out of state with you," she added.

"Of course I don't want to destroy Ethan getting to
play soccer or any other sport. But he's surely not into
all those yet."

"No, but he will be soon. He played soccer and T-ball
this year."

"You can give me schedules and we'll work it out
so he can play. But Saturdays and Sundays and alternate holidays won't be enough time. That's not sharing
him equally."

His words were quiet but held that same note of steel.
She looked away again, thinking about how she could
divide Ethan's time to Jared's satisfaction. "I don't know.
You move your headquarters to Santa Fe," she suggested. "Then we can work this out much more easily."

"I can't do that," he answered patiently. "It isn't the
air hub that Dallas is, or the oil center. Dallas is far more
accessible. If either of us is going to move, it would be
less of a hassle for *you* to move. Fort Worth is filled with
museums and Dallas and Fort Worth both have art galleries. You could work in either place and be close at
hand."

She laced her fingers together and thought about her
peaceful life in Santa Fe that had been simple in so
many ways, and about how Jared was going to
demolish all of it.

"Move to Dallas, live in a big city with all the traffic and hassle."

"There are quiet housing sections, both inner-city and suburban, old and new, with their own shopping areas and galleries. I can look into the best locations, Megan. I can buy the house you want or build it for you," he offered.

She closed her eyes and shook her head, tempted to cry out that she didn't want his money or support or interference.

"I don't know, Jared," she replied finally. "Leaving Santa Fe and all I've established and have there seems monumental. What about Ethan's friends?"

"Megan, he's six years old," Jared reminded her gently. "He'll adjust to anything you do."

Agitated, she stood and walked away from him, gazing at the flaming torches on the beach that shed bright circles of light on the white sand. She could see the tiny whitecaps washing on the shore's edge, the vast dark ocean beyond. Could she bear to move? If she didn't, she would have to pack Ethan up and send him off a great distance, whenever Jared saw his son.

If only she had sold Jared the ranch—what a bad decision she'd made!

Jared turned her to him. "If you move to Texas, it'll be much easier for us to share him. You know that. And there's no way I can move my headquarters and all my people to Santa Fe. Be realistic."

"Realistic! Give him up and tear my heart out is what you mean!"

"No, it's not," Jared replied firmly in a quiet, patient voice. "I keep telling you to share him with me. Megan,

I want what's good for him, too. You act as if you're sending him to some terrible fate."

"I know," she admitted. "I know you want what's good and you want to get to know him, but moving to Dallas is an idea I have to adjust to."

"That's the most workable solution. He could still participate in all the activities and you and I'd both be there to see him."

"What happens to him if you marry someone?" Megan asked. "She'll want to have her own children with you. She'll never love him like a mother."

"I'm not marrying anyone. That's not remotely on the horizon. Unless it's you."

"No. I'm not marrying without love. You'd be getting Ethan and convenient sex and I'd get my emotions too tangled up in a relationship."

"Look, just take life as it is now. Let's not take on additional problems.

"Stop fighting me, Megan. I can see it in your expression." His hands squeezed her shoulders lightly, kneading and massaging. "You're as tense as a spring that's wound tightly."

"There's no way this is something I can take lightly," she insisted. "Would a month in the summer work and maybe a week in the winter?"

"Not at all. Equal division. That's what I want," he replied and she took a deep breath, her mind running over possibilities and rejecting them as quickly as she thought of them.

"Let me consider it, Jared," she said, twisting away from him and walking farther out onto the veranda.

She stared out at the ocean and the silvery moon reflected in it while she pondered.

Jared's hands closed on her arms. "Megan, you're making this so damned difficult," he whispered, leaning near to trace kisses across her neck.

She turned to protest and looked up into his eyes. "No," she whispered.

"You don't mean it," he answered and leaned forward to silence any further protests with a kiss.

They died the minute his mouth covered hers. In spite of her intentions, all she could think was she wanted to make love once more with him.

She wound her arms around his neck and stood on tiptoe and kissed him fervently. With a groan, his arm tightened around her waist and he shifted to stroke her back, twisting free the few buttons.

"Meg, darlin', you'll never know how I want you," he whispered, pausing to frame her face with his hands and look at her. "With all my being," he whispered and kissed her again.

Faint tugs at her back made her realize he was unfastening her top. He peeled it away and leaned back to pull it free and drop it. He unclasped her bra, taking it off, and then he cupped her breast and rubbed his thumb lightly over her nipple.

Desire was a storm, as impossible to refuse. He was enticement, forbidden dreams, a danger to her peace. But he'd already destroyed that. Her hips rubbed against him in invitation. Her kiss caused his groan. There was no stopping or going back. She was as helpless as a leaf carried on a rushing current.

His fingers touched her waist, and in seconds her skirt fell around her ankles. She stepped out of it and her shoes as he leaned back to look at her, his leisurely gaze made her tingle. Eagerly, she tugged off his shirt and unfastened his belt and slacks to let them fall. As soon as he'd kicked them off along with shoes, she peeled away his briefs to free him. He knelt to pull a packet from his trousers and then he picked her up.

"Jared, this is a dream," she whispered, more to herself than him.

"It's a dream come true, Meg."

Clinging to him, she kissed him as he walked a few yards to place her on a chaise lounge. He moved between her legs and paused to put on the condom. Then he lowered his weight and she wrapped her arms and legs around him as he entered her slowly, driving her wild.

"Jared, love…" His kiss smothered her words and he kissed her as he eased out and then entered her slowly again, teasing and building need, until she arched against him and was writhing with urgency.

Perspiration beaded his shoulders and his forehead as he continued, and finally his control vanished and he thrust hard and fast. She crashed with a climax and rocked with him as he reached his, rapture enveloping her in a golden glow.

Sex was fantastic, but the wrong thing to happen in her life. She lay in his arms as he turned on his side and kept her with him. She caressed him, stroking his back, kissing his shoulder lightly.

"Meg, I want you here with me," he whispered

between the light kisses he showered on her temple and cheek. "Give us a chance and see what develops."

In a tropical setting, it was more difficult to cling to logic and remain cool and remote. She knew she couldn't trust him with her heart a second time. She had to go home.

He shifted, holding her close with one arm while he caressed her shoulder and brushed her hair away from her face. "You're beautiful. And this is the best."

She caressed his shoulder, kissing him lightly, momentarily enveloped in euphoria and wanting to stay that way a little longer. She wondered whether she would remember this moment all her life. Both of them nude, wrapped in each other's embrace on the sandy beach. A faint breeze came off the water and she could hear the splash of breakers as they rolled into shore. Lantern light flickered over Jared's face, illuminating his prominent cheekbones, leaving his eyes in shadows.

"We should shower," she said.

"How about a quick, moonlight dip? Pool or ocean?"

"Ocean," she replied and he stood to take her hand. They ran into the water, and when it was over their knees, both fell into it to swim. After minutes, he caught her and stopped, standing in waist-deep water to pull her to him and kiss her again. Their bodies were wet and warm, tantalizing to her. Her heart thudded and she was certain she had to go home to put distance between herself and Jared and get out of this magical dreamland setting where problems lost all reality.

Wrapping her arms around him, she kissed him. He

picked her up and waded out to the beach to carry her back into a bedroom.

They made love in bed, and afterward he held her close while he caressed her and murmured endearments that she barely heard. Her mind raced over what to tell him and when, deciding to let it go this night, and to deal with it in the light of day, which would restore a semblance of normalcy.

She wrapped her arms around him to hold him and kiss him again.

They loved through the night and finally slept in each other's arms, as sunlight began to tint the world with pink. In his arms, she thought about the future, deciding she would go home, mortgage the ranch and hire the best lawyers possible to fight Jared. That would throw it into the courts where the best lawyer usually won.

She woke to an empty bed and left to shower and dress in blue slacks and shirt.

As soon as she was dressed and ready, she sat by the open door to gaze at his tropical flowers and the ocean while she called the family accountant to get him to look into the best rates to mortgage the ranch. After a brief argument, he acquiesced and made plans, saying he would be prepared when she returned home.

Next, she called her South Dakota bank to check on the savings left to her by her father. Then she called the Santa Fe bank to check on savings there, then talked with her stock broker about what she could get from stocks and bonds.

She would have to find new lawyers, the best she

could hire. Jared would know the most competent, but she couldn't ask him. There was that billionaire client— he'd bought her pottery. He could probably give her sound advice. When she was back at the ranch and knew how much she would have available for a court fight, she'd get in touch.

She would have to go home and tell Ethan about his father. There was no avoiding that, so it might as well happen her way.

And she wanted Jared to have a day or two of full responsibility for Ethan, because as a confirmed bachelor, Jared might discover he didn't want to be burdened with a child after all, and all her problems would be solved. She couldn't imagine him enjoying being tied down to his son to the extent that he talked about.

Finally, she brushed her hair and put it in a thick braid. She found Jared in the kitchen with breakfast waiting.

He wore khakis, a white knit shirt and deck shoes, and he paused to look at her thoroughly. "Good morning. Come join me," he said, strolling to her.

She put up her hand and shook her head. "Last night was magic, Jared, but it's daylight, and reason rules now. I want to go home as soon as possible."

"Why? I thought we were gaining ground. We've talked about some options, developed a relationship, eliminated some possibilities—what's the rush?"

"I never intended seduction and lovemaking."

"You can't say it's been bad," he remarked.

"Of course not. But it isn't what I want and it isn't

doing my future any good. And I told you, I can't separate it from my emotions the way you can. I don't want to fall in love again."

"If falling in love occurs, I'd think it would be the best possible development. It would solve our problems."

"I don't trust you. At home we're in a regular setting, with a normal routine. Logic is not swept away by tropical breezes and magical nights. I want to be back where I can weigh the options for the future. And so far, I haven't found any I like, even if you have. This may have to get settled in court, Jared," she said.

His features hardened and a glacial look came to his dark eyes. She didn't care if he didn't like her answer. She hadn't liked any of his.

"Megan, don't make me take you to court. That could get really ugly and cause a world of hurt for all three of us," he said in a tone of voice that she suspected had made more than one grown man quail.

She shook her head. "You don't frighten me. I'll tell you what I want to do first. I want to go home and tell Ethan that you're his father. Then I want you to come stay a couple of days at my ranch and begin to get to know him. After that, if it looks feasible, and I approve, I want you to take him home with you and see how you like having responsibility for him all on your own," she said.

Jared's expression changed instantly. He came around the table and placed his hands on her waist. "Megan, absolutely fantastic! Now that's more like it.

I can get to know him and Ethan can get to know me and you can see us together. That's a terrific suggestion!"

"I thought you'd like it," she said, wondering if he thought he would win her over to doing things his way completely.

"Thank you, Megan. That's grand. It will give us time to bond. I'll call to get the plane ready and we can be on our way in about two hours. How's that?"

"It's fine with me, Jared."

He smiled at her and her pulse raced. He looked so damned appealing and sexy, and in spite of all her anger with him, she wanted his arms around her and she longed to kiss him.

But she had the wisdom to not do anything personal. Yearning and anger conflicted; she wanted him to back off. She knew she was in love with him a second time.

"We'll work this out to everyone's satisfaction. You'll see."

"It would be miraculous if it happened. I just don't see how."

He moved away and got his cell phone out of his pocket to make calls. She left him to get ready for the trip home, carrying her bag to the front door and sitting on the veranda to wait.

"Tell me about Ethan, and remember, I want a picture. I'd like to see your scrapbooks about him," Jared said as they flew home.

"Of course," she said, "although most of the scrapbooks and that sort of thing are in Santa Fe, not South Dakota."

"When I come to Santa Fe, I'll see what you keep there."

"Jared, you may find you don't want the responsibility of a child," she said, receiving a stormy glance and feeling their clash of wills that had returned full force.

"If you're counting on that, you might as well forget it. I'm going to try my damnedest to get along with my son and be a father to him."

"That's different than being a chum."

"I know that much. How soon will you get him home from your uncle's house?"

"I'll drive to Sioux Falls when we get back. I called while I was waiting for you," she said. "I told them I would pick him up today and take him to the ranch. You can come tomorrow."

"Did he mind the change in plans?"

"No. You said it yourself—kids adapt. He's looking forward to seeing me, and I'll be glad to see him. This has made me miss him twice as much."

Jared nodded and reached over to take her hand. "Thanks for what you're doing. I know you don't want to, but it's inevitable and much better this way, when you smooth the introduction. Anything we can do to make this transition easier will be better for Ethan, and I appreciate it."

"I might as well try to do things the best way for him," she responded, aware of her hand in Jared's, his dark eyes resting on her.

"I still want you," he said, sliding his hand behind her head and leaning forward to kiss her long and slowly.

She kept reminding herself to resist him, but she kissed him back instead. And each kiss forged a tighter bond, would be a bigger heartbreak and more of a struggle for her.

He raised his head. "Stop fighting me, Meg. You want this, too."

"No, I don't. I will contend with you as long as you kiss and flirt." She withdrew her hand from his. He stretched out his long legs and crossed them at the ankles.

"Tell me about Ethan," he said.

They talked about Ethan over a light lunch, and then Jared tried to charm and entertain her the rest of the way home with stories from his life.

Finally, she told him good-bye and headed to the ranch, anxious to see Ethan. And she wished with all her heart she didn't have to face her son and tell him that his real father wasn't who he'd thought all these years, but another man—one he had met only recently and briefly.

That evening, she pulled her son onto her lap. He was big enough that his legs dangled almost to the floor, but not quite. "Ethan, I want to talk to you about something important."

Eight

Thursday morning Megan opened the door and stepped back to let Jared enter. For the first time since he was in his early twenties, he was nervous. He held a package in his hand wrapped in plain gray paper. He also had a junior-size football and a paper sack. Even with all his thoughts on the event ahead, he noticed Megan. He wished they'd stayed at his Yucatán home another day or more, because he wanted more nights with her, and he'd already missed her badly. It was a surprise that he would want her with him so much because he had thought he was over her and she would no longer be so important to him. She had her hair in a braid today and she wore tight jeans, a green T-shirt and boots.

"I left my things in the car. I can get them later,"

Jared said and she nodded. "He's okay with all this?" Jared asked.

"Yes," she answered. Her eyes were wide, a clear turquoise, and she looked pale and somber. "He's curious and I think he likes the idea of having a dad, but he's shy."

"Where is he?"

"He's waiting in the family room. Jared, after I introduce you, I'm going to leave the two of you to get acquainted. I may go riding. It's a pretty June day and he likes to play outside, so that's good. You can take him out or you can stay in the family room. If you want to call, I'll have my cell phone. I'll stay out of the way for the next two hours."

He nodded. "That's great, Megan. I want to take both of you to dinner tonight."

"Thanks, but I already have steaks. We'll eat here and it'll be easier."

They entered the family room and he saw Ethan dressed in jeans and a T-shirt. He sat on the sofa playing with toy cars. As soon as they walked into the room, Ethan assessed him with a mixture of shyness and curiosity. He stood and waited.

"Ethan, this is Jared Dalton. You met in town last week. He's your real father. I told you about him."

Jared held out his hand to shake Ethan's. "I brought you a present."

"Before you open it, Ethan," Megan said, "I told you earlier, I'm going to leave so you and Jared can get to know each other. I have my cell phone and you know how to call me. I'll be back after a while." She leaned down and he ran to her, holding up his arms and she swung him up to hug and kiss him. He held her tightly until she leaned away to set him on his feet. "Be a good boy."

Ethan looked solemn and worried as she glanced at Jared. "I'll be back in a bit."

"Thanks, Megan." He turned to his son. "Ethan, I also brought you a football," Jared said. "We can throw it a little if you'd like to. First open your present."

Ethan nodded solemnly.

"Ethan—thank him," Megan prompted.

"Thank you, sir."

"You're welcome," Jared said, smiling at him, wishing he knew a way to make this easier for Ethan.

"I'll leave now." Megan walked away and Jared wondered whether she was crying or not. He looked back at Ethan. "You can open your present, Ethan."

Ethan slowly tore away the wrapping paper and opened the box to stare at the contents.

"It's a model airplane and it has a real motor. If you want, I'll help you put it together and then we can take it out and fly it."

"Sure," he said, glancing at Jared with a faint smile, and Jared let out his breath, thankful that it appeared he'd bought the right gift. Ethan looked in the box again and sat on the floor, starting to pour the contents out.

"Wait a minute, Ethan. I brought some things we'll use. Let's go out on the porch and work out there."

Ethan picked up the box and ran outside and Jared followed. "Ethan, I also brought a camera. May I take your picture?"

"Sure," he said, immediately halting and waiting.

Jared pulled a camera out of the sack and took three pictures.

"Can I take your picture?"

"Of course, here's the camera. Do you know how?"

"Yes, sir. Mommy showed me." Jared watched Ethan turn the camera in his small hands and hold it out, clicking a picture. He smiled and handed back the camera and Jared showed him the picture he had taken.

"Good job. When I get home, I'll print out copies and send them to you." Jared began to empty his sack, withdrawing a newspaper to unfold it. "Now, let's build the plane and fly it."

Ethan plopped down and helped Jared spread the newspaper. Next, Jared pulled out an instruction sheet and glue and a sheet of stickers from the sack and sat on the floor of the porch beside Ethan to work with him, letting Ethan do all that he could by himself.

He was surprised how well Ethan took directions, soon losing his shyness and working happily with Jared as if they had known each other for years.

"Mr. Dalton—"

"Ethan," Jared interrupted gently, placing his hand on Ethan's shoulder. "I'm your dad. Call me Daddy or Dad, whichever you like, but I'm not Mr. Dalton to you."

"Daddy," Ethan said shyly, staring at Jared, and Jared reached over impulsively and picked up Ethan to hug him.

"Ethan, I already love you. You're my son, my child, my baby even if you're not a baby any longer. You're part of me and my love is yours."

Ethan put his thin arms around Jared's neck and hugged him. "I'm glad you're here, Daddy. I've wanted a daddy because my friends have daddies."

"Well, you have one and I'm here to stay. If I had known I was going to be a dad, I would have come back immediately, Ethan. I won't ever leave you again except for short times when I go to work or you go to school," Jared said, feeling tears well up, surprised he was so emotional about Ethan. He hugged the boy's small, thin body and closed his eyes, holding his son close. "You'll never know how much I do love you, Ethan, but someday, when you're a daddy, you'll begin to understand."

Ethan laughed and wiggled to get free, so Jared set him back where he had been, beside the toy plane that was almost complete.

"We have to let this dry for about thirty minutes," Jared said. "Then we'll go fly it." He watched, helping when necessary, as Ethan did the finishing touches and then picked the colors he wanted and lined up the small pots of paint.

Ethan picked up a paintbrush, dipped it in green paint and began to apply it to the fuselage.

Watching as Ethan concentrated on painting his airplane, Jared marveled at how easily a child accepted life. Jared watched small fingers put on a coat of bright green paint, with orange flames along the cowling.

"Great plane, Ethan!" Jared praised his son as he rose to step back and take a picture of Ethan painting his toy model.

"Now, Ethan, we wait for it to dry," Jared said,

closing the pots of paint. "We'll clean up. And since I brought a football, we can go toss it, if you'd like."

"Yes, sir. I want a drink of water first."

"Okay, come with me to the kitchen."

Jared held the door and went inside the quiet, cool house, feeling Megan's presence even though she wasn't there, seeing her touches in a vase of cut red roses, seeing a book she was reading that was on the table beside a chair. If only she would agree to the marriage of convenience, or at least to move to Dallas, they could so easily share Ethan's life. Instead, from all she'd said, she was preparing to go to court, and Jared dreaded it. It would hurt all of them—a bitter, damaging battle. One he expected to win, which would hurt Megan even more.

If they went to court, though, he vowed to fight for full custody. She'd regret not cooperating with him. He could get better lawyers than she could, and more of them, he was certain. The whole prospect was dismal and distasteful. And so unnecessary. They'd had a wonderful night in the tropics. Megan was the most exciting woman he'd ever known, and since their return to South Dakota, he'd missed her terribly.

He poured Ethan a glass of water and watched the boy's small hands encircle the little glass. He was totally fascinated with his son, and thankful Megan had suggested they get to know each other right away.

As Ethan finished and handed the glass back to Jared, he cocked his head to one side. "Where's the football?" he asked, running toward the porch. Jared followed, stepping out to see Ethan already in the yard, tossing the ball up and then running to get it when it fell in the grass.

He turned to throw it to Jared, who had to leap to one side to catch it. Jared moved closer and threw an easy toss underhand, which Ethan caught with both hands. He beamed with pleasure, throwing it back toward Jared.

After ten minutes, Ethan tired of catch and ran to climb on his swing. "Come push me."

"How about a 'please'?" Jared asked, strolling over to swing Ethan.

The morning passed and they were flying the plane when Megan emerged from the house carrying a platter with sandwiches, which she put on the table on the porch. She came out to join them as Ethan called to her.

"Look, Mommy! Look at the plane I built. And it flies!"

"Good job, Ethan!" she complimented him, walking up to Jared. He watched her approach, and he longed to go take her into his arms and kiss her and thank her for the morning with Ethan. Instead, he stood quietly waiting, wanting her in his arms and in his bed again with an increasing urgency.

"Looks like you've won his friendship, which I knew you would," she said solemnly.

"Don't sound so disappointed," Jared said, annoyed with her tone—even as he desired her.

"I'm not. I know he needs a father in his life. I brought lunch, if either of you are hungry. Looks as if I may not be able to tear him away from flying his plane."

"He can come back to it," Jared said, turning to Ethan. "Ethan, land your plane and let's go eat lunch."

"Watch, Mommy. Watch my plane. Look at this," Ethan called, pressing buttons and toggling a switch on his remote control, bringing the plane to the ground with a bounce. Jared and Megan both clapped and she smiled.

"That's great, Ethan," she said.

He dropped the remote control and ran toward the table.

"Go wash your hands," Megan called after him, and he disappeared into the house.

"I think I'll do the same. We've had an assortment of activities this morning, and I feel dusty," Jared said, heading into the house behind Ethan.

They all reconvened on the porch to eat lunch, which Ethan wanted to escape after only a quarter of a chicken salad sandwich. Megan excused him and he ran off to play with the airplane again.

"So you bonded instantly. I'm relieved to see that you get along and can communicate with him."

Jared smiled at her as he sipped ice tea. "You're surprised and I would guess you're disappointed."

"Not really. I'd be unhappy if you couldn't."

"He asked me why I didn't marry you. I told him I asked you a few days ago and you didn't want to change the life you have with him right now. You may get questions yourself."

"I have, and I expect to get more. I try to be as up front with him as I can. Your answer was a stretch, because what you proposed was a marriage of convenience. Of course, that's the only kind it could be, because we're not in love."

He leaned forward to touch her cheek lightly. "It

doesn't mean that love isn't going to happen. It could occur if we both try to be friends."

"Forget it, Jared. I'm not marrying you and we're not going back to the way we were."

"I thought we got along great at my Yucatán home," he said.

"The time in the Yucatán was a rare moment that won't happen again. Let's drop it. Here comes Ethan."

Jared straightened and turned to watch Ethan, who came to sit with them and talk about his airplane. "Daddy, will you come fly it with me?"

"Sure will," he said, looking at Megan, who was frowning. "If Mommy will excuse us."

"Of course," she said, and Jared left with Ethan, who ran to jump off the porch steps, half-stumble and keep running to his plane. Jared watched him get the plane in the air. He thought about going back to help Megan clean up, but decided to stay out of her way.

After Jared had grilled dinner, they spent the evening in games with Ethan. Megan finally stood. "Ethan, it's bedtime. Say good night."

"Mom! School's out and I'm not sleepy."

"Give me a good-night hug, Ethan, and do what your mother says. The first thing you know, it'll be morning and we can fly your plane again," Jared said, pushing his chair away from the game table and standing to hold out his arms and pick up Ethan, who put his arms around Jared's neck in a hug.

"Will you come kiss me good night?"

Jared looked over Ethan's head at Megan.

"He can come kiss you good night in about thirty minutes. You have to have a bath and then I'll read a story to you," Megan said, reassuring him.

"All right. I'll be there in about thirty minutes from now. For the moment, good night, Ethan," Jared said, kissing Ethan's forehead. He set him on his feet. "Now go and get to bed so you can get up."

Ethan turned to scamper away ahead of Megan. "Well, thanks. Tonight he's cooperating fully with you and that makes my job easier." She left the room and Jared hoped she would return and sit with him in a while. He wanted to be with her. He missed her and their night together had been paradise. But the future wasn't going to be rosy if she was going ahead with what she'd threatened.

He moved to the porch and sat, propping his feet on the railing and staring out into the yard. Light from a lamppost shed light on a flowerbed, and faded into darkness beyond.

He glanced at his watch and headed toward Ethan's room. As he approached he heard the sound of Megan's voice. At the doorway of Ethan's room, he paused. Megan was stretched out in bed with Ethan beside her, and she held a child's book in her hand. She read quietly to Ethan, who was curled against her, his eyes barely open. One hand held his toy airplane and another held a frayed blue blanket that he fingered as she read. A battered white bear lay in Ethan's lap.

Jared entered and sat quietly in a rocking chair. She glanced at him, though Ethan seemed too sleepy to notice. Jared rocked and watched her. A small lamp burned and showed Megan beautiful in the low light. Her midnight hair spilled forward, glints shining in the cascade of thick, straight strands. Jared wanted her, but he was also held captive watching her, hearing the love and tenderness in her voice.

He knew whatever happened in the future, he could never take Ethan from Megan. All afternoon and evening love radiated between them constantly. When he'd been around her, Ethan had hovered next to her, touching his mother as if to reassure himself she was there. And she watched him with obvious love and pride in her gaze. Sadness swamped him that they were caught in a dilemma that could so easily be avoided if she would drop her bitterness over the past.

Jared realized he'd let her father intimidate him. He should have stayed.

In the end, right before he'd left, he had gone to his own father to let him know about Sorenson's threats. Jared could remember his father's rage and insistence that Jared stay and try to talk to Megan, but at twenty-five, after growing up watching the two men fight over every ranch problem that involved his neighbor, Jared had no doubts that Edlund Sorenson would carry out his threats.

At the time, deep down, he'd felt Megan probably had known what her dad was doing. He was her father, after all. If she didn't, Jared figured they would get back together, and shortly after he had gone, he wrote her the first letter. All his letters went unanswered, which to him, at the time, seemed an answer in itself.

She must have known some of what her father had done. He couldn't imagine Megan would condone her father harming his neighbor, but she had to have been aware of his acts throughout the years. Too many times, Sorenson had tried to take their water by damming up the river.

Both men always shot the other man's animals when they roamed on either of their properties after fences had gone down—his own father in retaliation. Occasionally hands from the Dalton ranch had had tires slashed in town, and they'd always blamed Sorenson's hands.

Also, Jared had known there was no use going to the police and telling them about the threats. Edlund Sorenson was respected in the community and it would be his word against Jared's.

His dad had been ready to fight, and wanted Jared to stay, but Jared was afraid for his dad, who was getting older and wasn't as strong as he'd once been. He didn't want his family hurt, so he'd left.

Waiting, Jared thought about the future. When she finished the book, Ethan had fallen asleep.

She picked him up and Jared stepped up to turn back the covers. She tucked Ethan into bed, gently moving his plane beside him on the bed before kissing him good night.

"My turn," Jared said. He kissed him, still marveling that he had a son and how easy it had been today to get to know him. He turned to walk out with Megan.

"He's great, Meg, and today was the best. He accepted me."

"I figured you'd charm him. He's happy to discover he has a dad. Part of it is simply envy, but so far, you're winning him over. Don't get too chummy, because it could hurt him later."

"That's in your hands," he said, as they returned to the family room and she crossed the floor to sit in a wingback chair. He sat nearby, facing her.

"I might as well tell you, Jared, I'm hiring a legal firm in Chicago. You'll get to see Ethan sometimes, but not half. I'll fight for that until the court takes him away from me."

"Megan, damn it, don't do this! It'll tear all three of us up. Ethan will be torn between us. I don't want to fight you over him. We can work things out if you give it half a try."

She shook her head. "No. Pack and go if you want to avoid a fight."

"I promised him I would never leave him. And I told him I didn't leave him the first time, that I didn't know about his birth."

"He told me what you said. Why don't you simply tell the truth? Admit that you got cold feet about marriage and walked out. He can take that as easily. It didn't involve him."

"I didn't get cold feet, Megan," Jared said with force.

She tilted her head to study him. "I don't even want to hear about it," she said, getting up and walking away. "I told you to come spend a few days to get to know Ethan, but I don't know that my nerves can take this, Jared. Tomorrow, take him home with you for a couple of days overnight and then bring him back. By then you two should know each other better."

Jared fought the urge to take her into his arms and

kiss away her protests. Instead, he crossed the room to put his hands on her shoulders and turn her to face him. "I want to take him home with me, but, Megan, drop this going to court. Rethink it…give us a chance to develop a workable relationship. Stop hanging on to anger from seven years ago," he said.

"That's easy for you, Jared. You're the one who wants all the changes."

"Yield an inch or two here! Try to cooperate," he said. He could feel the clash of wills, but desire was just as strong. Standing this close to her, looking into her thickly lashed turquoise eyes and at her full red lips that he knew were so soft, he was on fire with want. He pulled her to him, winding his hand in her hair and claiming her soft mouth. Fleetingly, he wondered if he was going to fall in love again with Megan, head for heartbreak twice himself.

Angered by her stubbornness, desiring her with all his being, he poured his raging emotions into his kiss.

Her hands shoved against his chest, but the push was brief and feeble, stopping as she slid her hands up and around his neck. And then she was in his embrace, pressed against him as he shook with eagerness.

He wrapped his arm tightly around her, leaning over her as he kissed her, thrusting his tongue deep into her mouth.

She kissed him in return, setting him on fire.

He wanted to pick her up and carry her to a bedroom, but he was afraid to break the tenuous moment; and holding and kissing her was better than having her tell him good night and send him on his way.

To his gratification, she responded, setting him ablaze. Finally she pushed forcefully against him and turned her head, ending their kiss. "Jared, you stop."

"You like me kissing you, Megan. Heaven knows, I like to kiss you more than any other woman I've ever known."

"Oh, Jared, please stop the shallow comments."

He wound his fingers in her hair as the other arm banded her waist, and he pulled her head back so she looked up at him. "There's nothing shallow about what I feel for you, and I meant exactly what I said. There's never been a woman in my life like you," he said solemnly, realizing that it was the truth.

"Jared, we're not going to sol—"

"A visit to Dallas is all I'm asking," he said, cutting her off and releasing her hair, then caressing her nape. "Bring Ethan with you. Will you come right away?"

"I'm going to regret it."

"That's a yes," he said with a jump in his pulse, because he saw a glimmer of hope of Megan cooperating with him. If she would come look at the Dallas-Fort Worth metroplex, with all the diverse lifestyles there, he thought he could win her over. Little by little, maybe she would work with him. "I can fly you there."

"I don't know about that," she replied cautiously.

"Nonsense. I'll fly us there. Plan to spend three days."

"Jared, I haven't said yes. I'll think about it."

"Bring Ethan with you and you'll see the possibilities."

"You're always a charmer, talking people into doing things the way you want them."

"And you're a seductress, setting me on fire." He

framed her face with his hands. "I want you, Megan. I want you and I want to work out things between us."

"I don't think we can," she answered.

"I know we can if we both try. Megan, are you scared I'll hurt him?"

"Heavens, no! Not physically, anyway."

"Then what are you afraid of?"

"I'm frightened you'll find him a fascinating diversion in your life for a while and then tire of the responsibility and care of a child and disappear out of his life. Children can't cope with that like adults can."

"No, I'll never do that," he said solemnly. "I love him too much to hurt either of you. I don't want a court fight over him."

"Words are easy," she said.

"I won't tire of him, either." Jared took her hand. "Come sit out on the porch and let's talk," he said, taking her hand.

She went out with him, sitting, watching him in the semidarkness as he pulled his chair close to hers. Light spilled through windows and the open door, dimly illuminating the porch.

"I'll show you Fort Worth. I can drive across Dallas if I have to and if you don't want to live close. Of course, close would be more convenient for both of us and make it easier."

"Easier for you," she said.

"Megan, I'm trying to find something workable," he reminded her.

"If I'd move to Dallas, would you back off having custody of him?"

Jared gazed at her. His first inclination was an imme-
diate no, but he waited, considering what she was asking,
but knowing that unless he was given legal custody,
Megan could easily keep him from seeing his son.

"No, because I don't think you'll always let me see him
otherwise. Let's not argue 'what ifs'. Just visit Dallas."

"I'll think about it," she said, standing. He stood at
once.

"Jared, be honest with Ethan. Don't tell him we're
thinking about moving to Dallas, because at the
moment, I'm not seriously entertaining the thought.
Santa Fe is home, and I have roots there now. Don't tell
him you want to marry me unless you think you can
make it clear to him that it's a business arrangement.
You'll get along better if you're up front and truthful."

"When haven't I been truthful with you?"

She shrugged. "When you declared you loved me."

"I did love you, Megan," he said, grinding out the
words, knowing his patience was stretching thin. He
caught her arms and pulled her closer and her eyes
widened as she placed her hands on his forearms reflex-
ively.

"Megan, I left because your father threatened my
dad if I didn't go!"

She closed her eyes and rocked back on her heels.

Nine

"Jared, don't! Don't lie to me," she said, hurting and angry at Jared.

"I'm not lying to you," he said in a tight voice, scowling at her. "Your dad warned me that he'd cut off water to our ranch and hurt my dad. He said he'd disown you and you'd be harmed in other ways, too. I may have made the wrong choice, but I still believe he would have injured my family terribly and you worse."

"If that's true, why didn't you contact me later and try to let me know?"

"We were threatened, Megan. I was a kid, and I left. I've paid for it a thousand times over."

"I don't want to hear this pack of lies, Jared!" she cried, jerking away from him. With every word he said, her fury intensified until she was shaking. "If he'd done

that, you would have come to me," she said, certain
Jared was lying and doing a poor job of it. "My father
was in such a rage about your disappearance—there's
no way he could have been the reason you left. Not
possible. I won't listen to such garbage!"

"Megan, I swear I'm telling you the truth," he said
quietly.

"I know my father better than that. You were head-
strong. Dad was a control freak and he interfered with
my life, but he wouldn't be that cruel. I know our dads
did dreadful things to each other, but neither ever did
bodily harm to the other. If he'd threatened you, you
wouldn't have listened," she said, disgusted with him.
"There's no common ground for us. This is hopeless. I
told you that you could take Ethan to your ranch and
I'll stick by my promise. Ethan can go home with you
tomorrow night. You leave with him early in the
morning and bring him back the day after tomorrow, on
Saturday, by dinner. Is that clear?"

"Megan, he threatened you. I don't know what else
to say," Jared said, clenching his fists. "I loved you and
it hurt to leave—"

"I will never believe you," she declared. "I don't
want to hear about it. Not anything. I'm going inside,
Jared. I'll see you in the morning." She walked past him
and into the house without looking back. She hated the
lies he'd told her. There was a dark side to him she knew
nothing about. She was surprised he would come up
with such a lame excuse. Yet she did know he could be
ruthless when he wanted something.

She prayed the legal firm she was hiring would get

what she wanted in a court battle. If they didn't, then she would try to bargain with Jared. If she lost badly in court, she'd look into moving to Dallas, but only as a last resort.

If only her pulse didn't still race with Jared's every look and her heart skip beats with his slightest touch. Right now, her nerves were raw and desire was a tormenting flame.

Ethan would be with him for two days. He had been good with Ethan, and they bonded instantly, which hadn't surprised her. When Jared was his charming best, he could easily win someone's affections. And Ethan wanted a daddy. Tears stung her.

She wasn't going into any marriage of convenience—one convenient only for Jared. She was already in love with him again. A marriage of convenience would devastate her emotionally. And he'd get the sex he wanted because she just couldn't resist.

He was in Ethan's life now, so she couldn't try to cut him out. Nor would she be able to legally, but hopefully, she could limit how much Jared would get Ethan.

She closed the door to her room and changed for bed, pulling on a robe, knowing sleep wouldn't come.

She left her room, stepping through the connecting door to Ethan's to look at him sleeping, serene and quiet. How she loved him! She could never regret knowing Jared, because he had brought her Ethan, the joy of her life. She smoothed locks of his black hair from his forehead, assured he would sleep through her light touches. Her love for Ethan had no measure, and she had to admit that Jared would make Ethan happy.

As he got ready for bed, he'd talked constantly about
his daddy and what they had done today. His toy plane
was still nestled beside him as he slept.

Was she being a fool to believe Jared again, when
he had broken her trust completely once before. He
had promised her that he wouldn't take Ethan from her,
and he'd promised Ethan he'd never leave him. Would
he really honor those promises? Tears stung her eyes
once again and she knelt and kissed Ethan.

"I love you so," she whispered, and then she turned.

Jared leaned against the doorjamb, watching her.

Glaring at him as he crossed the room to her, she
scrubbed her eyes furiously. Her emotions were in an
upheaval.

"Don't cry, Meg," he murmured. He picked her up
and carried her into her bedroom, shoving the door shut
behind him before setting her on her feet. He brushed
her tears with his fingers. "Don't cry. I don't want to
hurt you. He was happy today and you didn't lose a lot
of time with him. You let your aunt and uncle have him
for weeks."

Nodding, she firmed her lips, gazing up at him. He
had unbuttoned the first few buttons of his shirt and she
was aware of his bare chest, conscious of his hands on
her, memories of their lovemaking tormenting her.

Jared framed her face with his hands and gazed at
her intently. She couldn't keep from looking at his
mouth and wanting to kiss him.

His gaze lowered to her lips and she inhaled, her lips
parting and tingling. "Stop fighting me at each turn,"
he ordered. "You're making this damned difficult, and

it doesn't have to be." Jared's mouth covered hers and he kissed her. His arm slid around her waist and pulled her tightly against him as he kissed her, passion heating between them.

She ran her hand over his chest, feeling his groan.

He shook as he kissed her as he had before, and she was astounded by his need for her. She wanted him with an urgency that shocked her.

Reason prevailed and she pushed against him, finally leaning back. "Jared, we're not going to make love. I'm going to sleep alone tonight."

He raised his head and his eyes opened slowly. "I want you, Meg. I want you more than you can imagine."

"I'm not the woman for you. There's too much un-happiness between us. I can't tell you to get out of my life, but I'm not going to bed with you again."

When she pulled out of his embrace, he let her go. She walked away, going to the window. "Good night," she said.

In a moment she heard the door close and she turned to see that he had gone.

She put her head in her hands in frustration and anger. His story about her father had been appalling. She had never expected Jared to come up with such a lie.

She sat in a chair and gazed outside. Moonlight splashed over the yard, lighting broad areas, while beneath the trees was darkness. Near dawn, she dozed. And when she went into the kitchen for breakfast she found a note from Jared saying that he and Ethan had left for his ranch.

She wasn't hungry and went to her office to take care

of details regarding the new law firm, making arrangements to fly to Chicago overnight while Ethan was with
Jared.

Saturday, early in the evening, she waited on the
front porch with mounting excitement. She had missed
Ethan more each day. Worrying about him in a way she
never did when he was with her aunt and uncle, she had
tried to reassure herself often that Jared loved Ethan and
would take good care of him.

All the time they had been gone, she had promised
herself that as soon as Ethan was through with his visit
to Jared's, she would pack and return to Santa Fe. She
wanted to get back to the home that was a haven, and
far from Jared Dalton.

She saw the car approaching before she heard it.
Her eagerness mounted as she watch his black car wind
along the drive and finally stop. Ethan unbuckled and
climbed out, running to her and waving his arms, his
hands filled with toys.

She swung him up and kissed him while he hugged
and kissed her.

"Look what Daddy got me! I have another plane and
a car that will really run and I have a bigger car at his house
that I can ride around in on the patio. I have a new game."

"Good heavens! It's not even your birthday or
Christmas," she said, laughing at his exuberance as
Jared strolled up the steps. Looking too appealing, he
wore boots beneath tight jeans that rode low on his
hips. His navy Western shirt was partially unbuttoned,
revealing the thick mat of his chest hair. As his gaze

drifted over her, she became aware of her cutoffs, her red T-shirt and her hair in a braid. His unhurried gaze was as warm as a caress, and she tingled from head to toe.

"Thanks, Megan. We've had a great visit."

"I can tell."

"Want to go to dinner tonight? Or I can take you both to my place," he asked, as Ethan sat on the porch playing with his car.

"Thanks anyway, Jared, but we have plans."

He nodded. "I'll call you in the morning."

He looked at Ethan. "Ethan, tell me good-bye," Jared said, and the child jumped up to hug Jared, who scooped him up. He hugged and kissed him and she turned away to go inside the house. Tears threatened, and she hated that she got emotional so easily, where Jared and Ethan were involved.

In minutes, Ethan came running inside and she heard Jared driving away.

"Why couldn't we go eat dinner with Daddy?" Ethan asked, his brown eyes as intense as Jared's.

"We're going to get ready and go back home to Santa Fe," she said, something that usually Ethan was eager to do. To her surprise, he frowned.

"Is Daddy coming?"

"No, he's not."

"Can't we stay here so I can see him?"

"We'll be back here."

"Soon?" he asked, looking worried now. Megan frowned. Jared had already won Ethan's affections.

"Soon, I promise," she said. "If you want to."

"I want to. I want to see Daddy and he said he likes to be with me."

"I'm sure he does. So do I. Now let's get packed. It'll be for a week, Ethan, and then we'll talk about coming back here."

He nodded, but he didn't look any happier, and she wondered if her life was going to be in a perpetual turmoil because of Jared.

Jared drove away. The last two days with Ethan had been a delight with one flaw—he missed Megan. He'd hoped she'd come home with him tonight, or at least spend the evening with him, and he wondered what she was doing.

Each day that passed, he missed her more and he thought about her constantly. When he'd taken Ethan home, it had taken all his control to keep from crossing the porch and kissing her.

He wanted her badly. He thought about the marriage of convenience. It would be more than that, definitely no cut-and-dried business arrangement.

With his thoughts on Megan, he drove automatically, wondering what her plans were for the evening and why she couldn't go with him or if that had been merely an excuse. One certainty, she always responded when he kissed her.

At the thought of their kisses, he was aroused, tempted to turn the car around and go back.

She was important to him, necessary again. Years ago, after he'd left and she wouldn't answer his letters, he'd tried to get over his hurt. He'd wanted to drive her out of his mind as much as she was out of his life. Most of the time he'd succeeded to the point he felt she didn't matter. She was merely a part of his past. All through those years there had been a simmering anger. Maybe he actually had still been hurting. At the time, revenge had been a sweet idea. Had it really been revenge, or wanting to get her back in his life?

He realized he was in love with her again.

The truth shocked him, but then as he considered it, he knew it was love. He wanted to spend the rest of his life with her. Was there any way he could ever get past her anger? Perhaps there was one thing he could do. It could backfire or it could make a difference, but he was desperate with wanting her.

Megan waited until Sunday evening, when they were back in their home in Santa Fe, before she called Jared. The walled patio gave her complete privacy. Pots of bougainvillea and hibiscus bloomed in a riot of orange, pink and yellow. Potted palms and banana trees added greenery, and it made her glad to be in Santa Fe. Ethan worried her though, because he'd been uncustomarily glum.

Along with Ethan's, her own spirits had sunk. Had she made another mistake leaving South Dakota? She hated to admit that as furious as she was, she missed Jared.

She heard Jared's deep voice on the line. "Jared, it's Megan. I wanted to tell you that Ethan and I are in Santa Fe."

"You didn't give me any warning that you were leaving. Are you returning to South Dakota soon?"

"I don't know. I'll let you know if we do."

"I'd like to talk to Ethan. I was going to call him tonight."

"You can talk, but you won't be doing him any favors. He wasn't happy about leaving the ranch, because he wants to see you. You've managed to charm him, which I knew you would, and of course you've showered him with toys."

"Don't resent it, Megan. I have some years to make up—and I love him."

"You don't even know him!" she cried, and there was a long silence. "Jared, I'm sorry," she apologized. "That was uncalled for. I'm glad you love your son. My nerves are shot over this."

"You're causing a lot of trouble for yourself that's unnecessary, and you're going to cause yourself even more. Try to avoid catching Ethan in the crossfire."

"You're one to talk!"

"I've never deliberately hurt him. I didn't know about him, but then we're both aware of that."

There was another long silence and she started to say good-bye.

"Megan, write down this number." She picked up a pen and pad from the table beside her, figuring he was going to give her his Dallas office or home number.

"Go ahead," she instructed, then wrote the number, repeating it back to him. "Is this your home in Dallas?"

"No, it's not. Do you remember when your dad bought the ranch that adjoins yours to the north? I don't know how old you were."

Puzzled, she frowned. "I remember. I was a junior

in high school. The McGinnises moved away after their son's car wreck."

"That's right. Give Dirk McGinnis a call and ask him what prevailed on him to sell out to your dad and move out of state."

"Why…" she started to ask, but then bit off her words, going cold all over as she looked at the number on the pad in her hand.

"Megan, let me talk to Ethan. Please."

She barely heard what Jared said as her head swam. "Megan!"

His shout broke through, and she called Ethan, who came running and took the phone, walking away to talk to Jared. She stared at the number in her hands, knowing there was only one possible reason Jared would give her the McGinnises' number.

If her dad had made them move—threatened them or worse—then Jared had been telling her the truth.

She didn't have to make the call to have an answer, and she wasn't certain she wanted to hear the answer anyway. But if true, then it had been her father behind the breakup after all.

His treachery had been monumental. All along, it had been her father behind Jared's mysterious disappearance. Jared *had* left to protect his family.

She felt weak in the knees and had to sit quickly, as a light-headedness swept her. Through childbirth and the months of her pregnancy, her father had caused Jared to leave, and she'd been alone. Jared deprived of knowing his baby, their marriage plans in shambles, her heart broken—all because her father hadn't liked Jared or his family, and needed to control her life. She put her hands over her face and sobbed. Her own father hurting her so badly, being so cruel to them. She couldn't blame Jared for leaving.

"...I may have made the wrong choice, but I still believe he would have injured my family terribly, and you."

She hadn't known what her father had been capable of doing. She shuddered, shocked that she had been so incredibly wrong.

Error after error piled up with Jared, yet how could she have suspected her father's duplicity?

Her wrecked marriage plans, having Ethan alone, without Jared present at his son's birth or even knowing about it, her financial struggle, which had been unnecessary, a paper marriage—her father's cruelty had been monumental. And she'd cut Jared out of knowing about Ethan all those years. She owed him terribly to make up for all he'd suffered because of her father's unscrupulous ways.

Stunned, she barely heard Ethan when he came inside after he'd finished talking to Jared. Ethan seemed to sense something amiss and grew quiet through dinner. When Amy Brennan, his best friend's mother, called and asked Megan if Ethan could come to their house and sleep over, a rare treat, so Ethan and William could catch up, it seemed a blessing to Megan, and Ethan brightened immediately.

As she drove him to William's house, she glanced in the rearview mirror at Ethan. He sat buckled in the back, in his seat, with his new toy plane he'd brought to show William.

"Ethan, I think we'll go back to South Dakota sooner than I said. Would you like that?"

He brightened instantly. "Yes, I want to go. When?"

"Tomorrow, if we can get a flight."

"Awesome!" he cried, clapping and waving his arms, making her laugh for the first time in days. "Can I call Daddy and tell him?"

"Yes, but wait until you come home tomorrow," she said, suspecting she should have told him later. But he'd been glum since they'd left South Dakota.

Unable to stop grinning, he wriggled with eagerness. "That way, you can tell him when we'll arrive. I have to get our flight before we can tell him exactly when we'll be there."

Driving home she passed the red adobe buildings, turning into her quiet house. Pink, red and white hollyhocks bloomed in the yard and tall cottonwoods shaded her home and its double-thick adobe walls. She could see people milling on the porch to her gallery.

She returned to her house, to call Dirk McGinnis. She listened to how her father had threatened him and his family if he didn't sell. He'd refused to sell to her father, ignoring threats. Shortly afterward, his son had had a car wreck. The brakes had failed on his truck and he'd almost been killed. The young man still walked with a cane. There was nothing they could prove, but it had been her father, and she might as well know.

Weak-kneed again after she'd finished her call, she sat staring into space in the silent house. She owed

Jared the most profound apologies. There was no question she would share Ethan with him now.

Over breakfast, as the sun spilled over the thick adobe patio walls, she listened to birds sing, yet she felt as if the world would never be the same peaceful place she had known before.

As she cleared the table, the doorbell rang.

She glanced at her watch and frowned because it was only seven in the morning, and she couldn't imagine who would be ringing her doorbell.

She hurried to glance out the front window and saw a sleek, dark-green car in her drive. Anticipation churned in her as she rushed to the door to open it.

Ten

As if her wishful thinking had become reality, Jared stood holding an enormous bouquet of roses, lilies and daisies. Under his arm was a large box wrapped with a big bow.

"Jared! Come inside," she said, her excitement mounting. He looked handsome, solemn, fabulous and she wanted to throw her arms around his neck. Instead, she closed the door.

Jared turned to hold the flowers out. "I was going to send you flowers and then I decided I'd bring them myself. Megan, go to dinner with me tonight."

She laughed, feeling giddy in spite of a sleepless, worried night. "You surely didn't come to ask me to dinner." Her laughter faded. "Jared, I have to apologize to—"

He placed his fingers over her lips, and the instant he touched her, her heart thudded. He took the flowers from her and tossed them aside and dropped the package, taking her into his arms and leaning over her to kiss her.

Her heart missed beats as she wound her arms around his neck and clung to him.

While she kissed Jared, the walls she'd kept around her heart crumbled forever. She loved him and she wanted to work out whatever they could. And she had to apologize to him for doubting him and accusing him of lying.

"Where's Ethan?" he paused to ask.

"At a friend's house. Sleepover. We're alone."

Jared kissed her again and all else no longer existed.

He paused, framing her face with his hands and tilting her head up as he gazed into his eyes. "I had this planned differently, but I can't wait. Meg, I love you. I've missed you terribly and I love you."

"Oh, Jared!" she exclaimed, tightening her arms around his neck and standing on tiptoe to kiss him, stopping his words. His arm banded her waist and he leaned over her, kissing her fiercely, curling her toes and melting her knees.

Her heart pounded and she moved her hips against him, wanting him with all her being. He picked her up, still kissing her, finally raising his head. "Where's a bedroom?"

She pointed and pulled his head down to kiss him. Jared headed in the direction she'd pointed, and in a moment set her on her feet beside a bed as he pulled off her T-shirt and unfastened her cutoffs.

She fumbled with his clothing, peeling it away, and in a few seconds he was putting on a condom and moving between her legs.

She arched to meet him, hugging him and closing her eyes, already in ecstasy over his declaration of love. "I love you, Jared. Maybe I always have, and that's what made finding solutions so difficult."

He kissed away conversation, loving her until they both climaxed and finally lay locked in each other's embrace.

"I love you, Megan. The happiest times of my life have been with you," he said. "I made a mistake when I left. I should have listened to my dad, stayed and talked to you. I was hurt and angry and afraid for my family."

"Shh," Megan said. "We both made mistakes. I should have let you know about Ethan, because you would have come home. I had more wrong judgments than you did, Jared. I called Dirk McGinnis, but I knew when you gave me the phone number what I would hear. Actually, it was worse than I'd imagined."

"I'm sorry. I debated telling you, and I haven't all these years because I didn't want to turn you against your dad, and I didn't want to hurt you."

"It's all done. We've both erred and suffered for it."

"I'm not making a mistake now," he said, getting out of bed and picking up his trousers to come back and take her hand. "Will you marry me, Meg?"

Her heart thudded and happiness enveloped her. She threw her arms around him. "No marriage of convenience?" she asked with laughter.

"Hardly," he responded dryly. "Unless you call the past hour merely convenient."

"Oh, yes, I'll marry you, Jared."

He slipped a ring on her finger and she gasped in awe. "Jared, that's enormous!"

"You can select something else if you don't like it."

"Don't like it! Oh, Jared, this is so wonderful," she said. "This means you'll get me to move to Dallas after all."

"We'll see what we can work out so that we're both happy. I hate to take you away from here, if you love this. How about keeping this home, and you can come here when you want to?"

"When you come with me, you mean. I'm not letting you get far for long ever again in my life."

"I hope not," he replied solemnly. "Damn, I hope not. I love you, and you've made me the happiest man on earth."

She laughed. "I think that's my line to you."

"I'm getting you and Ethan, Meg. That's irresistible!" he said, pulling her to him for a scalding kiss, and all talk of marriage was gone for the next hour.

Later, she lay in his arms, their legs entangled while she looked at her ring, turning it so the light hit it at various angles. "Jared, are you sure you aren't marrying me to get my ranch?" He chuckled and she laughed, turning on her side to look at him. "Now it'll be yours, too."

"I told you I wanted it for a bet I have with two of my cousins."

"I remember. You bet Chase and Matt. I read about them in magazines almost as much as I did you. And if my memory is correct, they're each worth a fortune. I hope all of you made that loot honestly."

"And I hope you're joking."

"Of course I am. I'm deliriously happy. Tell me more about your cousins and your bet."

"We made a bet that we'd each put five million in the pot, and whoever makes the most money during the year will win the pot."

"Good heavens! You each bet five million dollars!" she said, sitting up to stare at him. "You didn't mention the amount."

"That's right," he said, caressing her bare breasts, and she grabbed the sheet which he promptly pushed away. She caught it once more.

"I need this or I won't hear one word you're saying. You expect to turn around and sell my ranch for a huge profit?" she asked in disbelief.

"Probably. It's one project of several that would bring a quick profit. What do you think about remodeling your ranch?"

She laughed again and shrugged, stroking his thigh. "Darlin', you can do anything you want to with whatever concerns me," she said in a sultry tone. He inhaled, pulling her to him to kiss her.

It was another hour before she sat up again. "Jared, I can't believe some of this. It isn't real."

"It's happening for sure," he said, rolling over. "One more item of business—plan this wedding as soon as possible. Money is no problem, so get the staff you need. I don't want to wait," he said, smiling at her.

She smiled in return, touching the corner of his

mouth. "I can't believe how happy I am. I agree. We'll have this wedding so soon that your head will spin."

"Let's get Ethan home to tell him," Jared suggested. "Isn't he young for a sleepover?"

"This is only the second time. His friend's mother and I are really close. And the two boys are, too. I thought it would cheer him up because he's been so glum about leaving you."

"I hate to say I'm happy about that, but I can't keep from being pleased that he's missed me."

"He's missed you, all right. We both have." She wrapped her arms around Jared's neck, clinging to him happily. "But first," she said, "there's some more loving to do here. We have years to make up, Jared."

"I'll try," he said, lowering himself to kiss her.

Epilogue

Megan gazed at her reflection in the mirror and felt as if she were in a dream.

"You look gorgeous!" her aunt said, smoothing Megan's cathedral train.

"Thank you, Aunt Olga," Megan replied, smoothing her pinned-up hair.

"I still can't believe you've pulled this all together in just weeks."

"Saturday, June, the twenty-seventh," Megan said, glancing at her watch.

"I need to go. The wedding planner called me in minutes ago. Jared said he'd watch Ethan. That child is so excited. I hope he doesn't lose your wedding ring."

"Ethan won't lose it," Megan said with a laugh, thinking about Ethan being their ring bearer. She walked over to pick up her enormous bouquet of white roses and white orchids from Jared. His simple note had read, "I can't wait…all my love."

"We'll be fine," Megan said, looking at her plain satin dress that was simplicity itself.

"Megan, it's time for you," the tall, brunette wedding planner, Stacy Goldman, said, opening the door. She helped Megan with her train as they walked to the foyer. Her hand rested on her uncle's arm as the wedding planner gave her the signal to start.

Megan's gaze went to the tall, handsome man who would soon be her husband. Her heartbeat quickened, racing with joy and love for Jared. He looked incredibly handsome, his black hair neatly combed and the black tux emphasizing his dark hair and eyes.

She loved him with all her heart—the lost years seemed nothing now. Jared was here and he loved her. In minutes he would become her husband. He was already Ethan's daddy, and they'd had the birth certificate changed to state the true parents.

As she drew closer to the altar, she glanced at Ethan, the ring bearer, standing beside his daddy. She smiled at Ethan and winked at him and he smiled in return, looking up at Jared with a big smile.

And then she was standing beside Jared, and her uncle placed her hand in Jared's. His warm fingers closed around her hand as the minister began to speak, but she barely heard the words. She glowed with love for Jared, so happy, knowing she was the most fortunate woman on earth.

Together, they repeated their vows, and finally they

took Ethan's hands and the three of them walked up the aisle together. They went out the door to go around to the back entrance to come back in for pictures..

"I love your mommy, Ethan," Jared said, swinging his son up into his arms and giving Ethan a hug and a kiss on his temple. "I love you. I love both of you with all my heart," Jared said, holding Ethan with one arm while he put the other around Megan's waist to hug her.

"I love you," Ethan said, hugging Jared's neck and then looking at his mom and reaching out to give her a hug.

They returned to the sanctuary to pose for pictures. Jared's dad was his best man, and his cousins, Chase and Matt, were groomsmen, plus Tony, a close friend from Dallas.

The reception was at Jared's ranch, where tents had been set up and tables were covered with food, including a six-tier wedding cake decorated with rosebuds and small pink orchids.

Jared took Megan into his arms for the first dance and she smiled up at him. "I can't believe I'm finally your wife."

"Believe it. I'll make it real for you if we can ever get away from here. I love you, Meg, darlin', and I'm going to tell you every morning and every night."

She laughed. "No, you won't! But if you do just some of the time I'll be happy. I think Ethan is as happy as I am."

"I hope so. God knows, I'm happy, Meg," he said, gazing at her with warmth. "Let's get out of here soon. They can all party without us."

"We will," she promised.

* * *

When the music stopped, Jared's dad claimed her for the next dance. Later Megan danced with Ethan, and halfway through Jared joined them, and the three held hands, smiling and dancing together.

"Here comes Chase," Jared said, and she glanced around to see his cousin approaching.

"May I have the next dance?" Chase asked, stepping up to take her hand. Jared and Ethan left and she danced away with Chase, his green eyes sparkling. "You've made him one happy man," Chase said.

"And he's made me a happy woman, Chase. And Ethan loves his daddy beyond measure."

"It's good for all of you, then, but I know it's good for my cuz. Megan, I don't want to bring up a bad time except to say one thing—Jared was brokenhearted when he left here. You'll never know."

"I can imagine," she said, looking toward the sidelines and seeing Jared watching her while he talked to Matt and friends.

"But that's over, and now he's so happy, he's goofy. And since it was our bet that got you two together again, it's even better, because he's too in love to win. He's so muddled right now, he's probably letting all kinds of deals slip through his fingers."

She laughed. "Don't count him out yet, Chase."

Chase grinned at her. "It's amazing how much Ethan looks like Jared. He's the spitting image."

"Yes, he is. He's so happy with Jared. Jared's already a good dad."

"He surprised me there. He's nuts about Ethan. I'm

happy for all of you," Chase said, gazing at her. "This is really great." He looked past her. "Here comes Matt for his turn to dance with you."

Megan turned, seeing thick black curls and blue eyes as Matt sauntered up to them and the dance ended. "You're rushing us," Chase said as Matt jerked his thumb.

"You've had your dance." He smiled at Megan. "May I have *this* dance?"

"I'd be delighted," she said, smiling in return. "Thank you, Chase," she said.

"My pleasure, Megan. Best wishes. And take care of him," he said, brushing her cheek with a light kiss.

"I intend to," she answered. Wind caught locks of Chase's straight brown hair and tumbled them on his forehead. He combed them back in place with his fingers as he walked away.

While a ballad commenced, she turned to Matt and they began to dance. "I hope you're both happy," Matt said. "Jared is, I know."

"Thank you, and I am, too. I love him."

"I'm glad you're in the family now. Of course, you know, now you'll have to attend Dalton family reunions and Christmas gatherings."

"That sounds wonderful. I like all the Daltons I know so far."

"Good thing. You're stuck with us now. Take Jared on a long, long honeymoon, and keep him out of Chase's and my hair. We've got unfinished business, and if you'll keep him busy, we can get a lot done without him."

"Could you be referring to a bet you made?"

He grinned. "Dang! He told you about our bet?"

"Yes, he did. Knowing Jared, he'll compete, honeymoon or not."

"Speak of the devil," Matt said and they stopped as Jared stepped up to take her hand from Matt.

"You guys go away. You've danced with her long enough, and Chase has had his turn."

"How you got her to marry you, I'll never know!" Matt teased, and Jared shook his head, taking her hand to dance away from his tall cousin.

"At last, I have you to myself again."

"Your cousins are charming," Megan said.

"You bring it out in them. Have I told you that you're gorgeous?"

"Yes, but I don't mind hearing it again," she replied, looking into his dark brown eyes and feeling the current that spun between them.

When the dance ended, they posed for more pictures and then cut the cake, and shortly after, she was separated from Jared as friends crowded around to talk to her about the wedding.

In the afternoon, Jared found her and took her hand and led her to the dance floor for another dance.

Jared danced her away from the crowd and around the corner of the house, then stopped. She was surprised to see her aunt and uncle standing there with Ethan, and she glanced at Jared.

"I told them to meet us here so we could tell them good-bye," he said.

She turned to hug her aunt and then her uncle. "Thank you both for all the help you've been. Thank you for everything and for keeping Ethan for us."

"You enjoy your honeymoon. Ethan will be fine," Thomas said, kissing her cheek.

Her aunt hugged her. "I'm so happy for you, Megan. I hope you have the joy that Thomas and I have had. Now don't worry about Ethan. We'll take good care of him."

"I promise, I won't worry." She kissed her aunt and then turned to pick up Ethan. "Give me a big hug," she said and hugged him in return.

He leaned back. "You'll come back and get me?"

"Yes. We'll be gone two weeks and then we'll come get you and take you with us for two weeks."

"Wow!" he exclaimed.

"Be a good boy."

"I will," he promised, and Jared lifted him to hug him. Jared reached into his pocket and pulled out a box that was wrapped in blue paper. "Here, Ethan, this is for you."

"Thanks, Daddy!" Ethan said, taking the box and ripping into it to pull out something folded up. Jared helped him unfold it, and a wire frame covered by a nylon net popped up.

"It's a bug cage, Ethan. Now you can catch a bug and put it in there and watch it. You'll have to feed it something or put some grass or flowers in the cage. After a day or two, let it go so it can go home."

"Thanks!" Ethan repeated, his eyes shining.

"We'll get going before we're missed," Jared said, taking her arm with another flurry of good-byes.

"Jared, what about your family? And I have to change clothes."

"I've already told my family good-bye, and I told

them we're slipping out. You can change on the plane. Your aunt gave me your dress and your things, and they're on the plane. Let's go." Holding hands, they ran to a waiting limo where Jared's chauffeur held the door for them.

She fell into Jared's arms, turning to kiss him, aware he had closed the partition to the front of the car and that they had privacy, with darkened windows.

"I love you," she finally said, raising her head. His hair was tangled over his forehead and he opened his eyes slowly, gazing at her with warmth in his expression.

"I love you, Mrs. Dalton."

"That sounds wonderful, Jared. I can't ever hear that enough," she said, smiling at him and tracing his lips with her finger as he smiled in return. "Now, where are we going?"

"To the airport. I have a seaplane that will fly us to Minnesota, to a cabin I bought on a lake there. We'll spend two days there and then we'll fly to my home on the Mediterranean. You'll like it. In two weeks, we'll come back and get Ethan, and we'll all go to Switzerland."

"Jared, this is a dream."

"No, it's real. I'll convince you of that today and tonight," he said in a husky voice.

"And how long before we get to that cabin in the woods?" she asked, running her hand across his chest.

"About two hours."

She groaned. "That's forever, Jared."

"I agree, but it's the best I could do, short of going to the hotel in town. We'll think of some way to make the time fly," he said, leaning down to kiss her again.

* * *

They finally were on the last approach, and the pilot landed on the ice-smooth surface of a brilliant blue lake. A man came out in a small boat to take them to the dock. Nestled in tall pines was a sprawling two-story chateau with a corral, barn and outbuildings.

"Jared, how many people live around here? And a cabin? This is a mansion in the woods!"

"There are a lot of people who work for me who have homes up here, and there are a few people who live around here all the time. It's an elegant cabin, I'll admit, but I don't care to rough it for my honeymoon."

At the door, Jared scooped her up to carry her over the threshold and set her on her feet.

She barely saw the house, glancing at polished oak floors, lots of pine and dark wood walls, but the minute Jared set her on her feet and closed the door, she turned to slide her arms around his neck. "Are we finally alone?"

"Yes," he said, drawing her to him. As she kissed him she could feel his fingers tugging free the long row of tiny buttons to her dress.

"Jared, you'll never know how much I love you and want you. I want to make up for all we lost. I want to kiss every inch of you, caress you, drive you wild," she drawled in a sultry tone, running one hand over his hip and winding the other in his hair. "You've always been the only man in my life."

"Ah, Meg, love. I've loved you since that moment on campus when you said hello to me. I don't think I ever really stopped loving you. I tried, but there was never anyone else I loved," he admitted, kissing her throat and ear, turning to cover her mouth with his until he paused. "I just didn't recognize what I felt for you."

His kisses were passionate, his lips warm on hers, and he shifted to caress her with one hand while he held her with his other arm. He pushed away her dress and inhaled, running his hands over her.

He raised his head. "You've made me the happiest man on earth, Meg."

She stood on tiptoe to kiss him, finally leaning away, "I love you and I want to make you happy always. Jared, this is so good," she whispered and then placed her mouth on his.

Her heart pounded with joy and she held him tightly, knowing they were a family now, and she would love him with all her heart for the rest of her life.

* * * * *

Don't miss Sara Orwig's next
STETSONS & CEOs *release,*
MONTANA MISTRESS
Available May 12, 2009
from Silhouette Desire.

Celebrate 60 years of pure
reading pleasure with Harlequin®!

Step back in time and enjoy
a sneak preview of an exciting anthology
from Harlequin® Historical with
THE DIAMONDS OF WELBOURNE MANOR

This compelling anthology features three stories
about the outrageous Fitzmanning sisters. Meet
Annalise, who is never at a loss for words… But
that can change with an unexpected encounter in
the forest.

Available May 2009
from Harlequin® Historical.

"I'm the illegitimate daughter of notoriously scandalous parents, Mr. Milford. Candidates for my hand are unlikely to be lining up at the gates."

"Don't be so quick to discount your charms, my dear. Or the charm of your substantial dowry. Or even your brothers' influence. There are as many reasons to marry as there are marriages."

Annalise snorted. "Oh, yes. Perhaps I shall marry for dynastic reasons, or perhaps for property or influence. After all, a loveless, practical marriage worked out so well for my mother."

"Well, you've routed me on that one. I can think of no suitable rejoinder." Ned rose to his feet and extended his hand. "And since that is the case, let me be the first to wish you a long and happy spinsterhood."

Her mouth gaped open. And then she laughed.

And he froze.

This was the first time, Ned realized. The first time he'd seen her eyes light up and her mouth curl. The first time he'd witnessed her features melded together in glorious accord to produce exquisite beauty.

Unbelievable what a change came over her face. Unheard of what effect her throaty, rasping laughter had on his body. It pounded a beat upon his ear, quickly taken up by his pulse. It echoed through him, finally residing in his stirring nether regions.

So easily she did it, awakened these sensations within him—without any apparent effort at all. And she had called him potentially dangerous? Clearly the intelligent thing for him to do would be to steer clear, to leave her to the tender ministrations of Lord Peter Blackthorne.

"You were right." She smiled up at him as she took his hand and climbed to her feet. "I do feel better."

Ah, well. When had he ever chosen the intelligent path?

He did not relinquish her hand. He used it to pull her in, close enough that he could feel the warmth of her. "At the risk of repeating Lord Peter's mistake and anticipating too much—may I ask if you'll be my partner in battledore tomorrow?"

Her smiled dimmed. Her breath came a little faster. His own had gone shallow, as if he'd just run a race— and lost. He ran his gaze over the appealing lift of her brow and the curious angle of her chin. His index finger twitched.

"I should like that," she said.

His finger trembled again and he lifted it, traced the

pink and tender shell of her ear, the unique sweep of her jaw. Her pulse leaped beneath her skin, triggering his own. Slowly he tilted her chin up, waiting for her to object, to step back, to slap his hand away.

She did none of those eminently sensible things. Which left him free to do the entirely impractical thing.

Baby soft, the skin of her lips. Her whole body trembled when he touched her there.

He leaned in. Her eyes closed, even as she stood straight against him, strung as tight as a bow. He pressed his mouth to hers. It was a soft kiss, sweet and chaste. And yet he was hot and hard and as ready as he'd ever been in his life.

She drew back a little. Sighed. Their breath mingled a moment before she slowly backed away.

"Oh," she breathed. Her dark eyes were full of wonder and something that looked like fear. He took a step toward her, but she only shook her head. His outstretched hand fell to his side as she turned to disappear into the wood. This was the first time, Ned realized. The first time, since he'd come to the house party at Welbourne Manor, that he'd seen her eyes light up.

* * * * *

Follow Ned and Annalise's story in May 2009 in
THE DIAMONDS OF WELBOURNE MANOR
Available May 2009 from Harlequin® Historical

Available in the series romance section,
or in the historical romance section,
wherever books are sold.

We'll be spotlighting a different series every month throughout 2009 to celebrate our 60th anniversary.

Look for Harlequin® Historical in May!

**60 years of Harlequin,
600 years of romance
in Harlequin Historical!**

REQUEST YOUR FREE BOOKS!

2 FREE NOVELS
PLUS 2
FREE GIFTS!

Passionate, Powerful, Provocative!

You're invited to join our Tell Harlequin Reader Panel!

By joining our new reader panel you will:

- Receive Harlequin® books—they are FREE and yours to keep with no obligation to purchase anything!
- Participate in fun online surveys
- Exchange opinions and ideas with women just like you
- Have a say in our new book ideas and help us publish the best in women's fiction

In addition, you will have a chance to win great prizes and receive special gifts! See Web site for details. Some conditions apply. Space is limited.

To join, visit us at
www.TellHarlequin.com.

The Inside Romance newsletter has a NEW look for the new year!

Same great content, brand-new look!

The Inside Romance newsletter is a FREE quarterly newsletter highlighting our upcoming series releases and promotions!

Click on the Inside Romance link on the front page of **www.eHarlequin.com** or e-mail us at insideromance@harlequin.ca to sign up to receive your FREE newsletter today!

You can also subscribe by writing to us at: HARLEQUIN BOOKS Attention: Customer Service Department P.O. Box 9057, Buffalo, NY 14269-9057

Please allow 4-6 weeks for delivery of the first issue by mail.

IRNNEW09

Harlequin® Historical
Historical Romantic Adventure!

> If you enjoyed reading
> Joanne Rock in the
> Harlequin® Blaze™ series,
> look for her new book
> from Harlequin® Historical!

THE KNIGHT'S RETURN
Joanne Rock

Missing more than his memory,
Hugh de Montagne sets out to find his
true identity. When he lands in a small
Irish kingdom and finds a new liege in the
Irish king, his hands are full with his new
assignment: guarding the king's beautiful,
exiled daughter. Sorcha has had her heart
broken by a knight in the past. Will she be
able to open her heart to love again?

Available April
wherever books are sold.

Silhouette Desire

COMING NEXT MONTH
Available May 12, 2009

#1939 BILLIONAIRE EXTRAORDINAIRE—Leanne Banks
Man of the Month
Determined to get revenge on his enemy, he convinces his
buttoned-up new assistant to give him the information he needs—
by getting her to *un*button a few things….

**#1940 PROPOSITIONED INTO A FOREIGN AFFAIR—
Catherine Mann**
The Hudsons of Beverly Hills
A fling in France with a Hollywood starlet turns into a calculated
affair in L.A. But is she really the only woman sharing his bed?

#1941 MONTANA MISTRESS—Sara Orwig
Stetsons & CEOs
It's an offer she finds hard to refuse: he'll buy her family's hotel—
if she'll be his mistress for a month.

#1942 THE ONCE AND FUTURE PRINCE—Olivia Gates
The Castaldini Crown
There is only one woman who can convince this prince to take the
throne. And there is only one way he'll ever agree—by reigniting
their steamy love affair.

**#1943 THE MORETTI ARRANGEMENT—
Katherine Garbera**
Moretti's Legacy
When he discovers his assistant has been selling company secrets,
he decides to keep a closer eye on her…clothing optional!

#1944 THE TYCOON'S REBEL BRIDE—Maya Banks
The Anetakis Tycoons
She arrives in town determined to get her man at any cost. But
suddenly it isn't clear anymore who is seducing whom….